To:

Riley

Eleanor
Pear

MELANIE ANN

A Legacy of Love

MELANIE ANN

A Legacy of Love

ELEANOR CLARK

HONOR ✠ NET

THE HONOR NETWORK

Dedication

O MY GRANDCHILDREN AND GREAT grandchildren. May you recognize, love, and appreciate your rich Christian heritage and the privilege of living in America, which was founded on the trust and hope we have in Jesus. May you continue the legacy.

Contents

Acknowledgments

*T*o my Lord and Savior, Jesus Christ, who has blessed me with the greatest family, life, and country. May every word bring honor and glory to Your name.

To my publisher, Jake Jones, who recognized the potential of my stories and my heart's desire to bless and encourage young readers to value their American and Christian heritage.

To my professor, Keith Whitaker, who encouraged me to write and taught me how to express my thoughts and feelings in print.

To my writer, Janice Thompson, who understood my love of history and breathed life into my stories with the skill of her pen.

To Annabelle Meyers who helped develop the character lessons.

And now abide faith, hope, love, these three; but the greatest of these is love.
—1 Corinthians 13:13 <small>NKJV</small>

Surely this weekend would be full of such stories—wonderful tales of adventure about the past.

A SPECIAL INVITATION

ELANIE ANN LOOKED OUT OF THE window as her mother pulled their car onto the familiar road. Recognizing her grandmother's neighborhood right away, she could hardly wait to get to Grand Doll's house.

"We're almost there!" the excited fourteen-year-old exclaimed. She tucked a loose strand of her long dark hair back into her headband. Then, clutching her grandmother's beautifully written invitation in her other hand, Melanie Ann looked down at the note one more time to read through it before they arrived.

Dear Melanie Ann,

A special weekend awaits you! Please arrive at my house on Friday afternoon after school. We will spend the next two days on a mysterious journey through time. Together, we will discover curious trinkets, secret treasures, and even timeless tales about the people in our family. We will share wonderful adventures together, I promise! Throughout it all, you will learn much about your family heritage and what it means to leave a legacy, especially the legacy of love.

I have chosen you for this very special visit because you are the oldest of all of the grandchildren. Soon, you will become "the keeper of the key." You will know what that means shortly. In the meantime, pack your bags, bring your adventurous spirit, and meet me in my living room on Friday afternoon promptly at 4 pm. Sir Splenda and I can hardly wait to see you!

Love and kisses,
GrandDoll

Melanie Ann folded the note again and put it in her backpack. She could barely wait to see her grandmother, and she also looked forward to seeing Splenda, Grand Doll's adorable little white Maltese dog. But what was all of this about mysteries and adventures? Did her grandmother have something up her sleeve? Was she being secretive on purpose?

Melanie Ann glanced over at her mom and smiled as she thought about the possibilities. She could hardly contain her excitement.

"Are you looking forward to this weekend?" her mother asked.

"Oh yes, very much," Melanie Ann responded with a happy nod.

"I have a feeling you're going to have lots of stories to tell when you come home."

"I'm sure I will," Melanie Ann said. Grand Doll loved to tell the stories of people in their family who had done wonderful things. And she always did so with a twinkle in her eye and great joy in her voice. Surely this weekend would be full of such stories—wonderful tales of adventure about the past.

"Be sure to take good notes," her mom said with a wink. "Your cousins will want to know absolutely everything."

"Oh, I will!"

Just about that time, the car turned onto her grandmother's street. Even from a distance, Melanie Ann could see the cobblestone driveway, its arching canopy of trees leading up to the large two-story home with beautiful columns, just beyond. She drew in a deep breath, and sighed. How wonderful it would be to live in such a glorious house! Grand Doll must surely love every minute of it, and how at home Melanie Ann always felt when she came for a visit.

"Grand Doll has the prettiest house in the world," Melanie Ann said as her mother turned the car into the driveway.

"I believe you're right."

Just then, her grandmother appeared at the front door with Splenda in her arms. She put the playful dog down on the ground, and he began to bark in excitement. Grand Doll gave a friendly wave, and Melanie Ann waved back, happy to be there at last. How beautiful her grandmother looked—tall and regal, with lovely white curls. And how her smile seemed to light up the whole street! That smile always made people happy and put them at ease.

As soon as the car came to a stop, Melanie Ann unbuckled her seatbelt and climbed out, then ran into her grandmother's arms. "Grand Doll!"

"Oh, I'm so glad you're here!" her grandmother said, giving her a warm hug and a kiss on the cheek. Her expression grew more serious as she asked, "Did you bring your invitation?"

"It's in my backpack," Melanie Ann responded with a wink. She knew how much her grandmother loved making visits special.

"Very good!"

Splenda jumped up and down at Melanie Ann's feet, anxious for some attention, so she reached down to pick up the little white fur-ball. He licked her all over the face, his tiny tongue tickling her, and she couldn't help but laugh. Afterward, he wiggled this way and that, nearly leaping out of her arms. Melanie Ann put him down, and he ran in circles around her feet. "I see Splenda hasn't changed a bit since I was here last," she said with a giggle.

Mother and Grand Doll struck up a conversation, and Melanie Ann went back to the car to fetch her backpack. Then, together, they made their way into the house.

"You will be in the luxury suite!" Grand Doll announced, pointing to the first bedroom on the right—a spacious, beautiful room with a tall antique bed and matching dresser.

"I really get to stay in here?" Melanie Ann asked in amazement. Many times she had seen the lovely guest room, but she had never slept in the large four-poster bed with its beautiful brocade comforter and pillows. Would she really be allowed such a privilege tonight?

"You will be treated like royalty all weekend," Grand Doll explained. "For that's what you are!"

Melanie Ann's mother laughed. "I'm afraid you might spoil her."

"Not a chance," Grand Doll said with a wink. "I just want to pamper my granddaughter a bit. No harm in that; she is a child of the King, after all! The day she asked Jesus Christ to come and live in her heart, she became royalty!"

Melanie Ann giggled, knowing Grand Doll was right, but still not feeling quite like a princess just yet. She put away her backpack and then turned to look at her mother and grandmother again. "What do we do first?"

"I'm afraid I have to leave soon," her mother said, glancing at her watch. "I have a meeting at church this evening."

Melanie Ann reached up to give her mother a hug and a goodbye kiss. "Don't miss me too much!" she said.

"I'll do my best," her mother replied with a wink. Then, after hugging Grand Doll, she headed off on her way.

Melanie Ann's thoughts quickly turned back to the hand-written invitation. She gazed up at her beautiful grandmother, and smiled. "So…," she said at last, "I understand we have some adventures ahead of us. I can hardly wait!"

"Indeed we do," Grand Doll said with a nod. "And if you are ready, we will dive right in!"

Melanie Ann followed her grandmother as they walked down the hall to the living room. There in the middle of the floor sat a large black trunk. Many times she had heard Grand Doll talk about the trunk, which had been brought over to America from Wales on a big ship in the 1600s, but Melanie Ann had never actually seen the trunk with her own two eyes. It was quite a sight to behold—covered in dings and dents, and looking rather worn.

"Wow!" she said. "This is it! This is the trunk with all of the family's priceless heirlooms and treasures!" She could hardly contain her enthusiasm as she stared at it in awe.

"It is," her grandmother replied, holding up a large tarnished key. "And I will open it so that we can have a peek inside. Then when we are done…," she said, giving Melanie Ann a serious look, "I will give you a key of your own, because one day this trunk will belong to you!"

"W…what?" Melanie Ann could hardly believe it. Could such a thing really be true? "The trunk will be mine one day? Are you serious?"

"Yes, that's right," Grand Doll said. "You can pass it on to your granddaughter. And she can pass it on to hers. So take a seat and listen carfully as I tell you about the items inside."

Melanie Ann dropped down onto her knees on the floor in the front of the trunk and watched in amazement as her grandmother slipped the key into the lock. All the while, Grand Doll hummed a little tune, one that sounded familiar to Melanie Ann. Perhaps she would remember what it was called before long. Right now, she was just enjoying listening. How her heart thumped in anticipation of what she would see inside the big black trunk! What wonders did it hold?

After a bit of twisting and turning, her grandmother finally pried the trunk open. It was filled with all sorts of things Melanie Ann had never seen before—a hand-painted teapot, a beautiful china-faced doll, a locket, an inkwell, and several photo albums, just to name a few. They all looked to be very old, like things you would see at an antique store, in fact.

"Oh, Grand Doll," she said, staring in wide-eyed wonder. "This is amazing. I've never seen most of these things before!"

"Well, listen closely," her grandmother said, "for each one has a story all its own."

Melanie Ann settled onto the floor, getting comfortable. She didn't want to miss a word of what Grand Doll was about to say.

"You will do great things for the Lord, sweetheart, and so will everyone in this family. Many will come to Christ because of you."

BREWING UP A STORY

*M*ELANIE ANN LOOKED ON WITH excitement as her grandmother reached into the trunk and pulled out a tiny teapot. It was quite beautiful—white and hand-painted with delicate pink flowers, with a little porcelain rose on the top handle. How dainty it looked! And how wonderful for preparing a hot cup of tea on a cold winter's day.

"Do you remember the story of this teapot?" Grand Doll asked. "It's very old. You once came to my house for a special tea party with your doll Chrissie, and I poured tea from this very spout!"

"Oh yes!" Melanie Ann exclaimed as she suddenly remembered a story her grandmother had once shared about a little girl in their family named Mary Elizabeth who had lived long, long ago. "Tell me again—how old is the teapot?"

"Nearly four hundred years old," Grand Doll explained. "This teapot came all the way from Wales to England to America in the 1600s, just like our family! It crossed the waters of the Atlantic and finally made it safe and sound—through hundreds of years and many, many families—to live in my house. It has been here since my mother gave it to me, and one day it will be yours!"

"I can't imagine it!" Melanie Ann gingerly took the teapot into her hands. "Really?"

"Really!" Grand Doll said, giving her a very serious look. "It traveled from generation to generation—from one country to another, then from one state to another. You could call this a traveling teapot. I've taken excellent care of it, and I know you will do the same."

Melanie Ann smiled at that.

"And who knows where it will end up one day? Why, maybe it will end up back in Wales before all is said and done—or maybe in Africa or even South America! Wherever our family goes, it will go!"

"That's interesting to think about," Melanie Ann replied. She opened the teapot and glanced inside, trying to imagine the dozens of people who had sipped cups of hot tea made in this very pot. She wondered where it might one day end up if she took care of it the way Grand Doll had done.

"Yes," her grandmother said, grinning, "isn't it fun to think that one day you will pass this little teapot on to *your* children and it will continue to pass from one hand to another?"

"Wow." Melanie Ann couldn't *imagine* having children of her own but didn't say so. Why, right now, she was having far too much fun just being a kid—playing softball, riding her bike, and catching fireflies at night. There would be plenty of time for grown-up stuff later.

Still, what if Grand Doll was right? Would she one day have a daughter or son, someone she could pass the teapot on to? Would her children one day hold the key to the trunk? Would they know the stories of their ancestors? Would *she* be the one to tell them?

Her grandmother's eyes lit up with great joy as she continued. "And *perhaps*, a hundred years from now, *another* grandmother and granddaughter will be sitting next to this trunk, pulling out this very teapot, talking about our family's rich history. Maybe *that* grandmother will share the story of Mary Elizabeth—the little girl who boarded the ship and made the journey to America. Or *maybe* that grandmother will tell a story of a girl named Melanie Ann, who grew up and worked as a nurse or possibly as a medical missionary in a foreign land."

Melanie Ann gasped as she thought about it. "You're right, Grand Doll. One day people will tell stories about *us*, the way you tell stories about our ancestors. We will be the people who lived 'way back when.'"

17

Was it possible? Would she really grow older like Grand Doll and pass on family stories? If so, she'd better learn all of them now so that she would tell them correctly! She wanted to be able to share them with the same twinkle in her eye as her grandmother did.

"That's right," Grand Doll said, "and what great stories our future generations will have to tell. All of my grand-children will leave behind a marvelous legacy; I just know it!"

"Oh, I hope you're right!" She closed her eyes and thought about the possibilities.

Grand Doll reached over and gave Melanie Ann a pat on the back. "You will do great things for the Lord, sweetheart, and so will everyone in this family. Many will come to Christ because of you."

With a smile on her lips and hopefulness in her heart, Melanie Ann nodded. She did her best to be a good witness—to others on her softball team and to friends at school. Would her grandchildren and great-grand-children really tell wonderful stories about her—like a character in a book—stories that made them smile? Stories that made them want to share the Gospel with others? Oh, she hoped so!

Melanie Ann ran her fingers across the painted flowers on the teapot. "It's just so hard to imagine this is nearly four hundred years old and that it hasn't broken yet!"

"Yes, praise the Lord!" Grand Doll said. "It's a very fragile piece of our family history, so we must be especially careful with it."

Just then, the little teapot slipped in Melanie Ann's hand, almost falling out. She grasped it tightly and whispered, "That was close!" Then she placed it back in the trunk and looked at it with curiosity. "I wonder what life was like in Wales," she said with a sigh. "Was it a lot different from our life here in America today?"

"Oh, from everything I have heard, it was quite beautiful in Wales," Grand Doll explained. "Our family came from an area near Laugharne Castle. I've seen pictures of it in a book and would one day love to visit, to see it with my own eyes. The area includes a beautiful green countryside with rolling hills and amazing blue waters along the Carmathen Bay."

Melanie Ann thought about that for a moment. "I don't get it," she said finally. "If it was such a beautiful place, why would Mary Elizabeth and her parents leave all of that to come to America? When you love someplace, why would you leave it?"

"Good question," Grand Doll said.

"I love my home, and I can't imagine ever leaving!" How hard it must be, to travel such a distance. And what about your friends? They would have to remain behind.

"Ah." Grand Doll's face grew more serious. "Our ancestors came to America for the same reason so many others came at that time—religious freedom. They were not allowed to worship God freely in their own country."

"Wow." Melanie Ann could hardly fathom such a thing.

"Imagine for a moment that you weren't allowed to pray or worship God as you wanted to," Grand Doll said. "Imagine the leaders of your country telling you that you couldn't go to the church you liked or tell others about Jesus. Imagine they said you would have to go to prison if you dared to witness to others."

Melanie Ann shuddered. "I can't even imagine that," she said, shaking her head. It sounded awful—all of it.

"In the 1600s, people all over the globe were facing religious persecution," Grand Doll explained. "Many were being put to death for their beliefs. I know it's difficult to relate to because we haven't experienced it very often in America, but things like that were happening frequently to the people who left Wales to settle here."

Melanie Ann's eyes grew wide. "Put to death?" Was it possible? Were people really told they couldn't worship the Lord as they pleased? That would be awful.

"Yes, and others were imprisoned. They spent their lives apart from their families—all because of their faith. That's why members of our family made the journey from Wales to England and then boarded a ship for America."

"I remember hearing about that ship!" Melanie Ann exclaimed. "It was called the *Assurance,* wasn't it?"

"It was!" her grandmother said. "Do you remember what life was like aboard that ship?"

"Crowded? And a lot of people got sick?"

"That's right." Grand Doll gave her a serious look. "People were willing to risk their lives to get to this new country—America. Sadly, many didn't make it. They died along the way. However, others arrived on the shores of Virginia and built homes and started new lives."

"I'm trying to guess what that was like," Melanie Ann said, closing her eyes. But as hard as she tried, she couldn't imagine what it must have been like to have traveled thousands of miles from her home to a place she'd never been—all so that she could worship freely. It just seemed…difficult.

"It sounds a lot like the Pilgrims who came to America by ship," Melanie Ann said, remembering what she had been taught in school.

"Oh my, yes!" Grand Doll exclaimed. "I love Thanksgiving and the story of the Pilgrims and the *Mayflower*. They boarded the ship in September of 1620 and made a perilous journey, finally landing in America in November. But that wasn't the end of their trial. They were unable to make adequate shelter on land before the winter set in so they had to continue to live on board the ship. After many months of cold, disease, and hunger, they finally moved ashore in March of 1621. It is said that 102 passengers plus the crew originally boarded the ship, but only 53 survived. They all endured many hardships to be able to worship God as they chose."

"Wow," Melanie Ann sighed. "I had forgotten about all the trials they suffered."

"It took a lot of perseverance to go through all of that," Grand Doll said.

"Perseverance." Melanie Ann echoed the word, then sighed again.

"What is it, honey?" Grand Doll asked.

"Persevering is…" Melanie Ann paused, then looked up at her grandmother before saying, "Hard."

Grand Doll gave her a warm smile, one that made her feel better right away.

"Oh, honey, I know," she said. "Sometimes it's hard to keep going, especially when you're experiencing tough times at school or at home. But remember, the Word of God says, *Blessed is the man that endureth temptation: for when he is tried, he shall receive the crown of life, which the Lord hath promised to them that love him.* That's in James, chapter 1, verse 12."

"Endureth temptation…" Melanie Ann whispered the words, then grew silent as she thought about them.

At that point, Grand Doll stood to her feet. "Follow me into the kitchen," she said, picking up the little teapot. "I think it's time to 'take tea' and enjoy some cookies before the story continues. How does that sound?"

"Yummy!" Melanie Ann said.

She followed her grandmother into the kitchen, marveling at all the stories one little teapot could hold.

Blessed is the man that endureth temptation: for when he is tried, he shall receive the crown of life, which the Lord hath promised to them that love him.

—James 1:12

THE LEGACY OF
PERSEVERANCE

ELANIE ANN LEANED HER ELBOWS on the white granite kitchen countertop and watched as Grand Doll brewed water to put in the pretty little teapot. All the while, her grandmother continued to hum the same familiar song. Perhaps Melanie Ann would remember to ask her about it later, once they'd finished looking through the trunk. For the moment, she wanted to focus on the tea and cookies!

"What flavor would you like?" her grandmother asked, pulling a box of teabags out of the cupboard.

"Flavor? Hmm, I don't know. What flavors are there?" Melanie Ann asked.

"Oh, so many!" Her grandmother pointed at the different colored tea bags. "Orange pekoe, chamomile, Earl Grey, peppermint…"

"Ooo! Peppermint tea!" Melanie Ann said. "That sounds great!"

As her grandmother poured the hot liquid into hand-painted demitasse cups, Melanie Ann couldn't help but wonder what it must have been like to live nearly four hundred years earlier, serve tea from this very pot, and drink from tiny, delicate china cups aboard a sailing ship. Had Mary Elizabeth also liked peppermint tea?

Grand Doll interrupted her thoughts with a question. "Would you like one teaspoon of sugar or two?" she asked.

"Two please," Melanie Ann said with a smile. She liked her tea sweet.

"That's just how I like it," her grandmother said, smiling back at her.

They settled down at the kitchen table, and Melanie Ann's mouth watered as she saw a plate of her grandmother's teacakes. She could hardly wait to have one. "These are my very favorites!" she said.

"Perfect for a mid-afternoon snack," Grand Doll agreed, putting two on Melanie Ann's plate.

As she nibbled on the yummy cookies, Melanie Ann paused every now and again to take a sip of the tea. Perhaps this was exactly how Mary Elizabeth had felt, sitting at a table with her mother in the 1600s. Maybe they had snacked on teacakes, sipped hot peppermint tea, and talked about what life would be like hundreds of years later. Did they know there would one day be a girl in their family named Melanie Ann who lived in Texas and that she would open the trunk they had brought over from Wales? Did they know she would enjoy "taking tea" with her grandmother? Melanie Ann laughed at herself. Or course they didn't. Only God knew that. Why, God knew *everything*!

"Would you like me to continue on with the story?" Grand Doll asked.

"Yes, please, Grand Doll, I would love to hear more stories about our family heritage," she eagerly responded.

"Well, let's see…," her grandmother said, pausing to take another sip of tea. "Mary Elizabeth and her family made it all the way to Virginia on the ship *Assurance*," she continued after a few moments, "but the hardest part was still ahead of them."

"No way!" Melanie Ann took another bite as she pondered that. Surely just getting to America was hard enough.

"Yes, they had to clear the land, build a home, and make it through a very harsh, cold winter." Grand Doll gave Melanie Ann a serious look as she said, "That's how life is sometimes. Just when you think the hard part is behind you, you find out there's more ahead. I've certainly discovered that in my own life. That's where perseverance comes in."

"I know what you mean," Melanie Ann replied, brushing crumbs off her fingertips. "Sometimes that's just when you feel like giving up. I found out the hard way during the softball season. Making the all-star team was great…at first."

"Oh?" Her grandmother's brow wrinkled as she bit into her cookie.

Melanie Ann nodded. "Well, the first few games were awesome—lots of fun. Just putting on my uniform and playing third base was a blast."

"Then what happened?" Grand Doll asked.

Melanie Ann shrugged. "After a while, I didn't feel like suiting up and playing anymore. I didn't want to put in all of the hours of practice. I was so tired. It was hot outside. And we weren't winning as many games as before." She remembered it clearly. Many of the girls on the team had grumbled. She certainly hadn't been the only one to complain.

"You were ready to give up?"

"Not really, I was just feeling left out," Melanie Ann sighed. "My friends—the ones who don't play soft-ball—were all having fun, going to the mall, the park, or the beach and doing other stuff together. And there I was—out on the practice field—hot, sweaty, and dirty. There wasn't much time left over just to hang out and relax. Sometimes, that's all I wanted to do."

"What if you had given up?" Grand Doll asked. "What would have happened?"

A smile came over Melanie Ann's face as she thought about it. "Maybe we wouldn't have won the championship. At least, I wouldn't have been there to be a part of it."

"Perhaps."

"I guess I never thought about it before," Melanie Ann added with a shrug.

"You are one of the best players on the team," Grand Doll asserted. "I've seen you with my own eyes. If you had given up, someone else would have taken your place, but it just wouldn't have been the same. What makes you good…" Her grandmother paused and took hold of Melanie Ann's hand before finishing. "What makes you good is that you stick with it, no matter what. You don't give into the temptation to run off to the mall with your friends when you should be doing something else. You don't stop trying, don't stop working, and don't stop believing you are going to be a success. Why, that's the very definition of perseverance—not giving up, no matter what!"

"Perseverance," Melanie Ann repeated. "What was that verse again, Grand Doll?

"*Blessed is the man that endureth temptation*," her grandmother quoted. "To *endure temptation* means to 'persevere under trial.' See, the trial was the part where you were growing weary and getting ready to give up. It was the part where you weren't always winning and you didn't feel like playing the game at all."

"I understand," Melanie Ann responded, nodding her head. "What's the rest?"

"*For when he is tried…,*"Grand Doll continued. But she then paused to add, "That's the hard part, going through the test. Seeing if you're going to pass or fail."

"I passed!" Melanie Ann said with a smile. "I lasted the whole season. I played every game and made every practice, even when I didn't feel like it. I did what my coach said. But what comes next?"

"The last part of the scripture says the person who perseveres *shall receive the crown of life, which the Lord hath promised to them that love him,*" Grand Doll said with a wink.

"So God rewards us for persevering?" Melanie Ann asked.

"Of course."

Melanie Ann thought about that for a moment before asking the question on her mind. "Was winning the championship my reward for not giving up? Is *that* what the scripture means?"

"Well, partly," her grandmother explained. "It's about living your life for God. About doing your best as a Christian and not giving up when times get tough. The ultimate reward is to be with the Lord in heaven one day. If we persevere through all the trials of life here on earth, we will one day walk on streets of gold in heaven. We will get to see those who have gone before us."

"Streets of gold!" Melanie Ann exclaimed as she finished off the last of her tea. She tried to imagine what heaven would be like. Would she really get to see it with her own eyes one day? And was it possible she would see and recognize her loved ones? How wonderful that would be!

"And those who have gone ahead of us—our grandparents, great-grandparents, and people like Mary Elizabeth—will be there to meet us."

Melanie Ann gasped. "You mean I'll get to meet Mary Elizabeth someday?"

Grand Doll smiled. "It's fun to think about, isn't it? All of the people throughout time who have put their trust in Christ, who have accepted Him as their Savior, will one day live together in heaven."

"Sounds really crowded!" Melanie Ann's eyes grew wide as she thought about it. How would so many people fit inside?

"According to the Bible, heaven will be quite large," her grandmother explained with a chuckle. "And think of all the people you will meet—the ones you've only ever heard about in stories. Kings and queens, presidents and dignitaries—all who have trusted Jesus as Lord will be there, not to mention your relatives from centuries gone by."

"Oh, Grand Doll!" Melanie Ann said. "Then tell me about more of them. If I'm going to get to meet them face-to-face one day, I want to know everything—absolutely everything—about them!"

Her grandmother laughed as she pushed back the chair and stood to her feet. "Well, come on back into the living room then. Looks like we'll be spending a lot of time going through the items in that old trunk tonight if you want to get to know all your relatives!"

Excited to hear more about the people she would one day meet, Melanie Ann rose from her chair and followed Grand Doll back into the room which held the precious, treasure-filled trunk.

Grand Doll smiled and then added,
"Wherever you go, God is already there."

DIPPING INTO
THE INKWELL

*T*HERE IN THE LIVING ROOM, MELANIE Ann settled onto the floor beside the aged trunk.

"What would you like to look at next?" her grandmother asked, peering inside. "Every item has its own story, so you may choose."

"Let's see…," Melanie Ann said, leaning over and looking curiously at the items inside. She lifted up a tiny glass bottle and gazed at it in awe. "What is this, Grand Doll? I've never seen anything like it." She rolled it around in her hand, giving it another look. Though it was quite small and delicate, it was stained on the inside.

"Ah. That's an inkwell." Her grandmother took it and gazed at it with a smile. "Before the days of ballpoint pens, people would fill these little bottles with ink, and dip their quills inside."

"What is a quill?"

"A quill is actually a goose feather. Many years ago, people would use a quill to write with."

"People wrote with feathers?" That didn't make a bit of sense to Melanie Ann. How could you write with a feather?

Grand Doll laughed and handed the inkwell back to her. "Well, folks didn't dip the feather end into the inkwell. They used the other end of the quill—the long, thin end. It made a wonderful pen."

"Wow." Melanie Ann wondered about the goose. Did he know his quills were being used as ink pens? If so, did he care?

"A quill didn't hold a lot of ink," Grand Doll added, "so it had to be dipped into the inkwell time and time again, especially if you were writing a lengthy note to a friend or family member. Remember, there were no telephones back in the 1700s, so people communicated by writing long letters. It was the best way to stay in touch."

"Oh, I see." Melanie Ann tried to imagine dipping a quill into the tiny inkwell, then writing a letter to a friend. It must have taken forever! Sounded like a lot of trouble, just to keep in touch with someone.

"People always kept an inkwell nearby when they were writing," her grandmother explained. "And remember, hundreds of years ago, people didn't have computers or even typewriters. Everything was written by hand, absolutely everything."

"Wow. No instant messages? No email? No text messaging on your cell phone?"

"That's right. All forms of communication were hand-written. And think about books and Bibles. People used to devote their lives to copying down the Holy Scriptures."

"Bet their hands got tired!" Melanie Ann said.

"Oh yes, but until the invention of the printing press, that is how the Bible was copied and handed down."

"We learned about the printing press in school," Melanie Ann said. "It was invented a long time ago."

"The first moveable type printing press was invented in 1440, by Johann Gutenberg," Grand Doll explained, "and he later produced the first printed Bible. It was called the Gutenberg Bible in his honor. But, of course, everyone still wrote by hand for many centuries after that."

"At school, we do a lot of things on the computer," Melanie Ann said. "I can't imagine writing everything down by hand. I'll bet, besides getting tired, their hands got messy from all of that ink." She stared down at her clean fingernails and tried to imagine what they would look like covered in sticky black ink.

"That is true. Why, people's fingertips were always covered in ink, especially those who loved to write," Grand Doll explained. "But their penmanship was excellent. These days, we rarely see such lovely handwriting. In the past, school children were taught to have great penmanship. They used quills and tiny inkwells just like the one you are holding in your hand."

"Really?" Melanie Ann thought about that. "So if I had gone to school hundreds of years ago, I would've had an inkwell on my desk? And a quill?"

"Certainly," her grandmother replied, nodding with a smile. "And a hornbook too."

"A hornbook?"

"Yes, a tablet to write down your letters and numbers. Most American schoolchildren had hornbooks to write on. Of course, they were hard to come by in Mary Elizabeth's time. In fact, they were still scarce when Victoria Grace came along over a hundred years later in the 1700s."

"Victoria Grace?" Melanie Ann set the inkwell on the floor and looked at her grandmother curiously. "Who was she?"

"Why, I believe I've told you about her. She was a little girl from our family who lived during the Revolutionary War. She was a courageous patriot."

"A patriot? What's a patriot?" Melanie Ann asked.

"A patriot is someone who cares very much about his or her country. Have you ever heard the word *patriotic*?"

"Yes."

"If you are patriotic, that means you love your country very much," Grand Doll explained. "It also means you are loyal to your country."

"I love living in America!" Melanie Ann said.

"Well, so did Victoria Grace. And she lived during a very difficult time—during a terrible war. But she was very brave. She worked as a nurse, tending to wounded soldiers."

Melanie Ann thought for a moment before she responded. "Oh yes! I do remember hearing about her," she said at last. "She was very courageous, wasn't she?"

"She had to be," Grand Doll said. "America was at war with England in the late 1700s. Victoria Grace's father went off to fight, and so did her older brother. But she remained at home with the rest of her family and continued on with her schooling. She wasn't very old at the time…not as old as you are now."

"And she worked as a nurse?" Melanie Ann's eyes lit up. "I want to be a nurse someday!"

"I know," Grand Doll said. "Perhaps you will take after Victoria Grace. That is her inkwell you were holding."

"Really?" Melanie Ann said. She could hardly believe it! "Maybe I *will* take after her," she said, "but my handwriting is terrible. I'd much rather type on a computer. I'm really fast on the keyboard!"

Her grandmother laughed. "Well, don't give up on writing the old-fashioned way. Spend more time with a pen or pencil in your hand, and you'll get the hang of it!"

"I guess it was really different, going to school in the 1700s. We have computers in our classroom and Internet access too. What did they have?"

"Their classroom was quite different. They had a pot-bellied stove in the middle of the room to keep things warm," Grand Doll explained, "and children of all ages attended class at the same time in that same room with the same teacher."

"Wow," Melanie Ann said, shaking her head. "I don't think I would have liked being together in one room."

"Oh, I don't know about that," Grand Doll said. "It's always fun to learn from those who are older, and it's even more fun to teach the younger children. Victoria Grace was an excellent student, one of the best in her class. In fact, she was the teacher's pet."

Melanie Ann couldn't help but smile. She was the teacher's pet too, though she would never say so.

"Dipping into an inkwell is a bit like dipping into your history," Grand Doll explained. "You never know what you're going to come up with!"

Melanie Ann giggled. "I see what you mean. Already, I've learned about two people from our family. But can you tell me more about what it was like to live during Victoria Grace's day? I can't imagine living in a place where a war was going on right in my own backyard!" A shiver went down her spine as she thought about it.

"I'm sure it was very frightening," Grand Doll replied. "But as I said, Victoria Grace was quite brave. Her faith was strong because her papa had taught her a scripture about courage from the book of Joshua. Do you remember that one?"

"I'm not sure," Melanie Ann shrugged. "Could you remind me?"

Her grandmother smiled. "Joshua 1:9 says, *Be strong and of a good courage; be not afraid, neither be thou dismayed: for the* Lord *thy* God *is with thee whithersoever thou goest.*"

"Oh, now I remember it," Melanie Ann said after she had heard it.

Grand Doll smiled and then added, "Wherever you go, God is already there."

"That's so interesting to think about," Melanie Ann said. "Sometimes it's hard for me to figure out how God can be everywhere all at once."

"Yes, He's everywhere. And He won't leave us or forsake us, even in the scary places—like during times of war."

"I've been watching the news," Melanie Ann said, frowning. "Seems like there's always a war going on someplace in the world. I wish it didn't have to be like that."

"Oh yes. I've lived through several wars myself," Grand Doll said.

"Really?"

"Yes. When I was just a little girl, our country went through World War II. Then, a few years after I was married, the Korean War came along. After that, the Vietnam War, the Gulf War, and then the Iraq War. I've seen many young soldiers go off to battle and prayed many prayers that they might return safely."

"Wow." Melanie Ann paused as she thought about that. "Some of the older boys in my neighborhood are in the Army or the Navy."

"Many others are in the Air Force, Marines, and even the Coast Guard or National Guard," Grand Doll added. "Why, we have fighting men and women all over the world. They face so many challenges. Imagine how brave they must be."

"And their families too," Melanie Ann said. "Joey Peterson—he's a boy from the down the street who's been gone for months, fighting a war on the other side of the world. His mom goes to our church, and she always asks us to pray for him. I try to remember to do that, but sometimes I forget."

"Mrs. Peterson sounds like a very courageous woman," Grand Doll added. "She must know exactly how Victoria Grace felt."

"I hope I'm that brave when I grow up," Melanie Ann said.

Grand Doll smiled. "You don't have to wait until you're grown. You can start right now."

"I can?"

"Of course!"

Melanie Ann reached into the trunk and pulled out the inkwell once again. Clutching it in her hand, she thought about the scripture Grand Doll had quoted. *Be strong and of a good courage; be not afraid, neither be thou dismayed: for the Lord thy God is with thee whithersoever thou goest.*

Yes. She would start right now. Why, if Victoria Grace could be courageous, surely she could be too!

Be strong and of a good courage;
be not afraid, neither be thou
dismayed: for the Lord thy God is
with thee whithersoever thou goest.
—Joshua 1:9

THE LEGACY OF COURAGE

*M*ELANIE ANN HELD ONTO THE inkwell and closed her eyes, trying to imagine what it must have been like during the Revolutionary War with gun blasts going off all around. Why, she could almost smell the smoke from the musket fire!

She thought about the men who had been called upon to fight, especially the younger ones. They had fought for a cause they believed in—to be free from British rule—and their bravery had led the way.

A shiver ran down her spine as she thought about the wounded soldiers that must have needed tending to. Surely many had been young, probably not much older than she was.

"That's it!" Melanie Ann said, opening her eyes. "That's what I would have done if I'd lived in the 1700s!"

"What is that, honey?" Grand Doll asked.

"I would've been a nurse just like Victoria Grace." Her words began to speed up as her excitement grew. "You know how much I love taking care of people when they're hurt or sick, so that's exactly what I would have done. I would have bandaged their wounds, given them medicine, and made sure they were comfortable. I would have offered them sips of water and broth, and done just what the doctor said to do. And I wouldn't have quit, even if I'd been afraid. Taking care of others *makes* you brave."

"There is a lot of truth to that," Grand Doll agreed. "Remember when your Grandma Grace got sick and you were the one who wanted to help out?"

"Oh yes!" Melanie Ann felt tears rush to her eyes at once. Why, after all, it had just been last year. She had worked to help care for Grandma Grace for several months right before she passed away. Those had been the hardest months of Melanie Ann's life, months she would never forget as long as she lived.

She could still remember her grandmother lying sick and frail in the bed, her soft white curls against the pillow. She could still hear the doctor's voice saying it would just be a few weeks before her grandmother went to be with Jesus. She remembered the tears of the others in the room.

Oh, how Melanie Ann remembered.

But she remembered something else too. She remembered the look of bravery in Grandma Grace's eyes and the courage in her voice as she said, "I'm ready to go to heaven, honey. I've lived a good, long life serving Jesus, and I'm ready to meet Him face-to-face, to walk on streets of gold, and to see those who have gone before me."

Melanie Ann would never forget how her grandmother's eyes glistened as she spoke those words.

Immediately, Melanie Ann had volunteered to help. "Please let me help you care for Grandma Grace," she had whispered to her mother.

"Are you sure?"

"Yes, please. I really want to take care of her."

And so she had. While her friends were enjoying after-school activities, Melanie Ann had spent her time in a small room at Grandma Grace's house, helping with medicines, putting clean sheets on the bed, and giving her sips of water. She had read books to her grandmother and brought her food. She had even cleaned up when messes were made.

She hadn't minded the trouble, not really, because she was learning so much—and spending time with someone she loved. Though her work there was very difficult, Melanie Ann wouldn't have traded it for anything in the world. During those months, she really got to know Grandma Grace, to spend special quality time with her. She would never regret that.

On the final day they were together, Grandma Grace reached for Melanie Ann's hand and gave it a squeeze. "You're a wonderful girl, Melanie Ann," she'd whispered in a soft, shaky voice. "The love of Jesus shines in your eyes. One day I will see you again, but until I do, you go right on loving others and tending to their needs. Promise me?"

"I promise," she had whispered.

Grandma Grace passed away later that night, but Melanie Ann had never forgotten her parting words. In fact, every time she thought about them, her desire to become a nurse grew stronger.

Just like Victoria Grace.

She smiled as she thought about it. "I guess I never thought about the fact that you *have* to be courageous when you're caring for someone who's sick," Melanie Ann said. "I've done that a few times in my life."

"And you've done a wonderful job of it," Grand Doll said.

"It hasn't always been fun," Melanie Ann admitted with a sigh.

"I think it's especially hard when you're caring for those you know and love," Grand Doll said. "And when they're really sick, like your Grandma Grace was, you know their time on earth is short. They are going to be with Jesus soon. It's bittersweet."

"Bittersweet?" Melanie Ann wasn't sure what her grandmother meant by that.

"Yes." A tear rolled down Grand Doll's cheek. "That means there's a sweetness, because you get to spend time together—but there's also a sadness, because you know the time is short."

A lump rose to Melanie Ann's throat, and she pushed it back. She didn't want to cry, but she couldn't help it. As the tears slipped down her cheek, Grand Doll drew close and wrapped her in her arms.

"Do you know when I think it's hardest to be brave?" she asked.

"W…when?" Melanie Ann reached up with the back of her hand to brush away the tears.

"Right after you've lost someone you love." Grand Doll's eyes misted over. "When my wonderful mother went to heaven, it was hard because I missed her so much!"

"Oh, Grand Doll, I'm so sorry."

"Being separated from someone you love is tough." Her grandmother flashed a warm smile. "But when Mama went to meet Jesus, it was also exciting because I knew that one day I was going to see her again in heaven!"

Melanie Ann smiled and nodded. "I think about that all the time. When I get to heaven, I'll see Grandma Grace, and I know she's going to be healthy and strong. She won't be in a bed. She won't be sick. She'll be able to run and jump and turn in circles and do all the things she used to do when she was young."

"That's right," Grand Doll said. "And I'm looking forward to that day myself. So is your grandfather."

Melanie Ann's eyes flooded with tears once again as she thought about her grandmother's words. "Oh, Grand Doll, that's hard to think about! I don't want to lose you and Poppie too!"

Grand Doll gave her hand a warm squeeze and looked tenderly into her eyes. "But, honey, don't you see? For those who put their trust in Christ, death is nothing to be feared. Why, believers get to spend eternity with their heavenly Father. When you've asked Jesus to forgive your sins and to come and live in your heart, you are His forever—not just here in this life—but in heaven too!"

At once, Melanie Ann felt peace in her heart. "I know you're right, Grand Doll, and I'll do my best not to be afraid anymore."

"Every time you start to feel even the tiniest bit fearful, just quote that verse," her grandmother said. "Don't ever forget it. *Be strong and of a good courage; be not afraid, neither be thou dismayed: for the Lord thy God is with thee whithersoever thou goest.* Joshua 1:9 is a legacy I want to leave to all my children and grandchildren—the legacy of courage."

As Melanie Ann continued to clutch the tiny inkwell, she whispered the verse, believing it with her whole heart.

No matter what happened—whether it was war on the other side of the globe, sickness in the family, or troubles with friends at school—she would always do her best to be brave like Victoria Grace. And like Grand Doll.

"*I know she trusted God with the changes she went through. I can trust Him with my changes too.*"

A GOLD LOCKET

ELANIE ANN BRUSHED AWAY HER tears and leaned over once again to look inside the large black trunk, more curious than ever about what she would find next. It seemed the more she learned about the people in her family, the more she wanted to know!

As she looked through the items, something caught her eye. She reached down and picked up a lovely gold locket, about the size of a large coin. On the top of the locket, two tiny gold friendship birds stood beak to beak. On the bottom of the locket were three small diamond chips. "Oh, Grand Doll!" She stared at the beautiful keepsake, unable to say anything else. Who could have owned such a beautiful thing?

"Open it and look inside," her grandmother suggested.

Melanie Ann tried to open the locket, but it was stuck. She tried again, but it would not open.

"Oh, we must get it open!" Grand Doll's brow wrinkled. "There are two photographs inside that you really must see!" She took the locket in her hands and worked with it until it suddenly popped open. "Ah! There they are!"

She handed the little locket back to Melanie Ann, who stared at the tiny photographs inside. They were faded and worn. Why, she could hardly figure out who—or what—they were.

"See that little girl on the right?" Grand Doll asked, pointing.

"Sort of." If Melanie Ann tried really hard, she could almost see the face of a little girl in the faded photograph.

"That's Katie Sue. She was born years and years after Victoria Grace. Her family lived in Tennessee, but her papa longed to move to Texas to settle on a nice piece of land and to start a new church."

"Texas? They came here?" Melanie Ann's eyes widened.

"Yes, and aren't you glad they did! If our family members hadn't moved here, perhaps you would have been born in a completely different place!" Grand Doll explained. "Katie Sue's papa decided to head west, so the family packed up everything they owned, including this black trunk, loaded them in a Conestoga wagon, joined a wagon train, and set out on the trail to Texas. Texas was a pretty new state when Katie Sue and her family arrived in the spring of 1852. In fact, Texas had only joined the United States as the twenty-eighth state in the Union seven years earlier in 1845.

But Katie Sue's family had a long journey before they even got to Texas—and what adventures they faced along the way!"

"They traveled in a wagon train?" Melanie Ann asked. "Like in the movies about the Old West?"

Grand Doll nodded, her face lighting up with excitement. "Yes, they traveled with several other families. The wagons lined up, one behind the other, as they journeyed from Tennessee to Texas. It took months to get here."

"Months?" Why, Melanie Ann could hardly believe that! Who would have the patience to travel for months on end? "It would only take a couple of hours if we flew from Tennessee to Texas on a plane," she said.

Her grandmother laughed. "Well, that's true, but you have to remember, there were no planes back then."

"Ah. That's right."

"In fact, there were no cars, no buses, nothing like we have today. So they traveled several hours a day just to go a few miles at a slow pace," Grand Doll continued. "And, of course, they'd stop at night, all of the wagons gathered in a circle, where there would be a campfire and sometimes singing and fiddle-playing. Katie Sue's father was quite the fiddle player. And from what I've heard, her mama was a terrific singer."

"That part sounds like fun," Melanie Ann agreed.

"Oh, I'm sure it was. Music has always been an important part of our family's history, so I'm certain Katie Sue's parents really enjoyed that part too. I'm not so sure her mother liked traveling by wagon, though. It would be really hard if you had small children."

"That's true," Melanie Ann said. "I learned a lot about wagon trains in history class. Lots of people traveled west in wagons back in the 1800s. Isn't that right?"

"Yes, it was the only form of travel until the railroad came along, and Katie Sue wasn't looking forward to the trip. She was just a little girl, but she made a very long journey. She truly didn't want to go—not at first, anyway. She didn't want to leave her home in Tennessee because her best friend Matilda lived there." Grand Doll pointed to the other faded photograph. "That's Matilda."

Melanie Ann squinted to see. "Oh, she looks pretty."

"They were best friends, and they didn't want to part ways. But Katie Sue had to learn to trust God for all of the changes in her life. That's not always easy."

Melanie Ann nodded and sighed. Seemed like the older she got, the more her own life kept changing. "I know how she felt," she said finally.

Grand Doll flashed a warm and loving smile. "I know you do, honey. But there's a wonderful scripture that always helps me when I'm struggling to trust. It's Proverbs 3:5–6: *Trust in the LORD with all thine heart; and lean not unto thine own understanding. In all thy ways acknowledge him, and he shall direct thy paths.*" She continued, saying, "I learned that verse in Sunday school when I was really little, and I've never forgotten it."

"I'll bet Katie Sue had that scripture memorized by the time she got to Texas," Melanie Ann said.

"No doubt." Grand Doll's face grew quite serious. "She had to face all sorts of dangers along the way—sickness, exhaustion, and hunger, just to name a few. And as I said, it took months to make the journey. Can you imagine how weary she grew?"

"Yes."

"Trusting God is something that we have to deal with every day, isn't it?" Grand Doll added.

"Yes, especially when everything around you is changing," Melanie Ann said. She sighed. "I'm fourteen, Grand Doll. *Fourteen.* It seems like everything in me is changing at once. I've grown four inches, just this year. My hair is changing. My skin is changing. And my shoe size is changing—my foot is three sizes bigger in just two years! Can you believe it?"

"You're growing up," her grandmother said with a smile, "becoming a lovely young lady. Of course, you will go through physical changes, but there are emotional changes as well."

"I know. Sometimes I just cry for no reason. And other times, I'm moody. My mom says she doesn't know what to do with me sometimes, and I'm not sure either!" Wondering how her grandmother would respond to that, Melanie Ann let out an exaggerated sigh and reached over to scratch Splenda behind the ears.

"That's not unusual for a girl your age," Grand Doll said with a smile. "I remember being fourteen. Change can be really tough."

"Yes, and changing from elementary school to middle school was especially hard," Melanie Ann said. "New teachers, new subjects, new friends, new grading scale, new sports, new everything. And starting high school. That was probably the toughest of all."

Her grandmother chuckled. "And just think…as the years pass, you will face even more changes!"

Melanie Ann groaned. "Does this changing thing ever stop?" she asked.

Her grandmother laughed. "No, honey. One thing in life you can always count on is change. You'll one day change from being a student to being a wife. Then a mother and then a grandmother. And in between, you're sure to change jobs too. You will live in different places, eat different foods, and get to know new people all along the way. Why, life is just full of changes!"

"It makes me tired, just thinking about it!" Melanie Ann leaned back and looked at the locket. "And a little scared."

"As scary as climbing in a horse-drawn wagon and riding all the way from Tennessee to Texas to a home you've never even seen before?" Grand Doll asked.

"No." She had to admit, that sounded pretty frightening.

"Our ancestors went through major changes in their lives," her grandmother explained. "And they made it! Their courage and their faith in God got them through."

Melanie Ann stared at the faded photograph of Katie Sue. "I want to be just like her," she said at last. "I know she trusted God with the changes she went through. I can trust Him with my changes too."

"Would you like to keep that little locket and wear it so that you don't forget?" Grand Doll asked.

"Oh, could I?"

Grand Doll drew close and gently took the necklace. Then, carefully opening the clasp, she slipped the chain around Melanie Ann's neck and fastened it. "There you go. Now you will never forget. You can trust the Lord, no matter what!"

"I can." Melanie Ann nodded as her fingers touched the delicate locket. She quoted the scripture once again. "*Trust in the LORD with all thine heart; and lean not unto thine own understanding. In all thy ways acknowledge him, and he shall direct thy paths.*"

As long as she wore this necklace, she would never forget that God was trustworthy.

Trust in the Lord with all thine heart; and lean not unto thine own understanding. In all thy ways acknowledge him, and he shall direct thy paths.
—Proverbs 3:5–6

THE LEGACY
OF TRUST

$\mathscr{M}$ELANIE ANN FINGERED THE LOCKET and thought about everything her grandmother had told her so far. What amazing stories she had heard. Oh, how she wished she could have met all of the girls she had discovered in those exciting tales! Surely they would have been great friends.

Mary Elizabeth sounded just wonderful. Best of all, she had persevered as her family traveled across the world by ship to their new home, and she had never given up. Victoria Grace had been really brave, helping injured soldiers during the American Revolutionary War. And Katie Sue sounded like a very special girl, one who went through lots of changes in her life yet kept her trust in God.

All in all, the girls in her family seemed—why, they seemed almost too good to be true. Were all of the people in her family that…wonderful?

"May I ask you a question, Grand Doll?" Melanie Ann asked after thinking about it a bit more.

"Of course!"

"Well, you've told me about so many of the girls in our family, and it seems like they were all great people who trusted in God. Were there any who didn't? Anyone who made mistakes? Anyone like…me?"

"Oh, honey…," her grandmother said, smiling. "I'm sure there were plenty of folks in our family who lost their way, who did wrong things. The Bible says in Romans 3:23, *For all have sinned, and come short of the glory of God.* We all make mistakes and do things we regret." Her face lit up at this point, and her voice grew more animated. "But isn't it interesting to realize, the stories that have been passed down in our family are all about people who loved the Lord and lived good lives? *Those* are the people who left a legacy. We don't know as much about the ones who drifted away from God, but we have a clear picture of those who relied on their heavenly Father to see them through the hard times. Those who were filled with trust—like Katie Sue, for example— have left a wonderful legacy."

"What's a legacy, again?" Melanie Ann asked.

Her grandmother's brow wrinkled a bit as she thought about it. "A legacy is like an inheritance. Think of it as a treasure that you pass down from one generation to another."

"Wow. So all of those people—the ones who trusted God—left me a treasure, an inheritance?"

"Yes, that's right!" Grand Doll smiled. "And here's the greatest part: you can leave a treasure for your children too."

"If I persevere?"

"Yes, and if you're brave and you continue to trust God through all of the changes you go through. When you live your life like that, you give people plenty to talk about!"

Melanie Ann chuckled. "I sure hope people remember the *good* things about me and not the bad."

"Oh, the good far outweigh the bad," her grandmother said. "That's obvious. And you're a girl who loves the Lord with your whole heart, so I know people will one day tell amazing stories about you. Here's the key—you must trust God not only with the little things but with the big things too."

Melanie Ann didn't say anything for a moment as she pondered her grandmother's words.

"Think of it like this," Grand Doll said. "Remember when you were a little girl and you wanted to learn to swim?"

"Yes ma'am." Melanie Ann nodded, but she wasn't sure what this had to do with trusting God.

"I remember watching you," her grandmother added. "You would stand on the edge of the pool, and your daddy would be down in the water with his arms stretched out, ready to grab you."

Melanie Ann smiled as she remembered. "Yes, he wanted me to jump into his arms."

"Did you trust your daddy to catch you?"

"Well…" Melanie Ann giggled a bit as she admitted the truth. "I knew he would catch me, but I was still a little scared. It was hard to make that first jump."

Grand Doll nodded. "See, that's what putting your faith in God is like. Even when you're not sure how things are going to turn out, you have to be willing to leap into your heavenly Father's arms. That's what trust is all about. He's a big God, and He can handle everything that you can't. He will catch you every time, just like the scripture says: *Trust in the LORD with all thine heart; and lean not unto thine own understanding. In all thy ways acknowledge him, and he shall direct thy paths."*

"That makes sense!"

"Yes, and here's the other wonderful thing. Once you're in the water, He can teach you how to swim. In other words, your trust will grow deeper and stronger, the more time you spend with Him. *But* you have to get in there before it can happen."

"I've learned so much from you, Grand Doll," Melanie Ann said. "Sometimes I think you're the smartest woman I've ever known."

Her grandmother laughed. "Oh, honey, I appreciate those words, but I can assure you, I still have a lot to learn. Even though I've learned to trust God—to jump into the water—I still struggle sometimes too. We all do."

Melanie Ann looked back at the old black trunk, thinking of all the things she'd discovered inside it. What a wonderful weekend this was turning out to be. She could hardly wait to tell Mama and all of her cousins about the adventures that Grand Doll had shared.

Melanie Ann ran her fingers along the edge of the trunk and smiled. "One day I will be the keeper of the key," she whispered. "*Keeper of the key!*"

With a grin, she looked back up at her grandmother, ready for another exciting story. Another adventure, as Grand Doll called it.

"Yes, you have to keep your light shining bright, and that means following God's commands and letting others see—in your words and your actions—that you are a Christian. All the time. No matter what!"

LET YOUR LIGHT
SO SHINE

ELANIE ANN LOOKED INTO THE trunk with great curiosity. "What happened next in our family, Grand Doll?" she asked. "Who came after Katie Sue? Somebody really amazing, I'll bet!"

She grew more excited as she thought about it. Who would it be? Someone who led expeditions to the Wild West? Someone who discovered new lands? Someone who helped others through difficult times? Oh, surely it was someone who left a wonderful legacy like Katie Sue and the other girls she had heard about.

Her grandmother's eyes lit up with joy as she answered. "Oh yes! One of my very favorites came next—Sarah Jane Powell. What a wonderful girl she was! I think you really would have liked her. She was a lot like you in many ways."

"Sarah Jane? Did she travel west in a covered wagon like Katie Sue?" Melanie Ann asked, anxious to hear more about her.

"Oh no!" Grand Doll exclaimed. "Sarah Jane was from a very well-to-do family from Philadelphia, Pennsylvania, and was expected to behave like a lady at all times!"

"Yikes! I guess she didn't play softball, then."

"No, though she probably would have liked to. She was expected to be very prim and proper, but it didn't seem to come easy for her! Sarah Jane and her parents traveled in carriages and private train cars, not covered wagons. They dined on fine foods, not chuck-wagon suppers like Katie Sue and her family."

"I'll bet it would be fun to be wealthy," Melanie Ann said with a giggle. "Sometimes I like to pretend!"

"I'm sure it was especially fun back then," her grandmother explained. "The clothes worn by little girls were so beautiful. And the hats! Why, fancy hats with feathers were quite the fashion."

"I don't think I'd like to wear a hat," Melanie Ann said. "A ponytail will do just fine for me, or a headband. Even a baseball cap is better than a fancy hat!"

Grand Doll laughed. "I don't blame you, but I'll bet you'd like to live in a home like Sarah Jane's. From what I understand, her family lived in a big, beautiful house near the center of Philadelphia, and her mother did a great deal of entertaining. They had a lot of parties in their home—high-society parties, for famous people—when they weren't traveling, that is."

"Did Sarah Jane live during the 1850s like Katie Sue?" Melanie Ann asked.

"No, she was born in the late 1870s," her grandmother said with a smile, "after the Civil War ended. It was a very interesting time in our country's history. The North and the South had been divided for years over the issue of slavery, but by the time Sarah Jane came along, some of those wounds were starting to mend. And by then, railroad tracks were going in all across the country."

"I heard all about the War between the States in school," Melanie Ann said. "It was so sad—brother fighting against brother. That's what my teacher said."

"Oh my, yes. The Civil War was certainly a dark season in our history. Did you know that the Civil War resulted in almost one million deaths? That's more deaths than all of the U.S. wars combined!"

"Wow, that's terrible!" replied Melanie Ann. "I never knew that part."

"The war lasted from 1861 to 1865, and about four million black slaves were set free. In 1862, President Abraham Lincoln wrote an executive order called the Emancipation Proclamation, declaring the freedom of the slaves; however, they were not all set free until the end of the war."

"Slavery was a terrible thing," replied Melanie Ann.

"Yes. Thankfully that awful season in our history came to an end. Then after the war, many people settled in the Philadelphia area, so it was quite the place to be!"

"I would love to go to Philadelphia one day," Melanie Ann said. "My history teacher told me all about it. Benjamin Franklin, the great inventor and politician, lived there, and so many other famous men and women."

"Philadelphia is also the home of the famous Liberty Bell," Grand Doll said with a smile. "I've seen it with my own eyes!"

"And Philadelphia is home of Independence Hall. My teacher called it the 'birthplace of the republic.' It's where the U.S. Declaration of Independence was written as well as the Constitution and the Bill of Rights!" Melanie Ann added, remembering her history lessons from school.

"The Bill of Rights was certainly an important addition to our U.S. Constitution," replied Grand Doll. "Those ten amendments, which limited the power of the federal government, were designed to protect U.S. citizens. My favorite is the First Amendment because it established the freedom of speech, press, and religion."

"That doesn't surprise me," smiled Melanie Ann. "I know how you love to tell a story."

Grand Doll chuckled. "Well, that is certainly true. That is why I love Philadelphia. Can you imagine how wonderful it was for Sarah Jane to live in such a place, filled with adventure and rich history? But my favorite story about her is the one where she and her family took the train to New York to see the unveiling of the Statue of Liberty."

"I've seen the statue in pictures on the Internet!" Melanie Ann said. "It's huge! There's a staircase inside, and you can climb up really high, all the way to the torch, I believe."

"Yes, I've been inside it," Grand Doll replied, nodding. "But can you imagine being there on the day it was unveiled? There were parades and parties and people from all over the world, celebrating from one end of New York to the other. Sarah Jane's family was right in the center of it all! Now, that was a girl who really knew how to let her light shine."

Melanie Ann looked up at her grandmother curiously. "Let her light shine? What do you mean, Grand Doll?" she asked.

"Actually, I have a picture that might help explain what it means to let your light shine." Her grandmother leaned over and looked inside the trunk. Locating a small blue photo album, she said, "Let's take a look in here. There's a picture I'd love to show you if I can find it…" One after the other, Grand Doll flipped through the worn pages of the album. Finally, she came to the picture she was looking for.

Melanie Ann could hardly believe it! "Is that you?" she asked, pointing to the black and white photo of a little girl dressed up as the Statue of Liberty.

"Yes," her grandmother affirmed, smiling as she stared at the picture. "Patriotism, a love for my country, was born in my heart when my school teacher asked me to play the part of the Statue of Liberty."

"Were you excited?"

"Oh my, yes!" Grand Doll exclaimed. "I was beside myself with joy!"

"Tell me about it," Melanie Ann pleaded.

"Well, I was about ten years old. We were studying American history, and the members of my class were acting out special events." She took on a dreamy-eyed look as she explained.

"Ooo! Sounds like fun! And you were chosen to dress up as the Statue of Liberty?" Melanie Ann questioned.

"I was! And you will never believe how honored I was to be asked to play the part of that special lady. Mother curled my hair like Shirley Temple's." Grand Doll smiled as she remembered. "She made me a white costume from a white sheet, and the torch I held was a flashlight under a white napkin."

Melanie Ann glanced at the photo again and smiled. "Sounds like a lot of fun."

"Oh, it was," Grand Doll said, "and I learned so much too! Our teacher explained that the statue had become a friend to the world because she was holding freedom's torch for millions of people."

"Wow!"

"And here's the best part," her grandmother said. "My mother explained that, as Christians, we should let our lights shine just like Lady Liberty. We need to hold our torches high. That's why I love the story of Sarah Jane so much. After she visited the Statue of Liberty, she learned a great lesson—that letting her light shine, or being a good witness, was very important."

Melanie Ann smiled. "You're right. I would have liked her!"

Grand Doll nodded. "There's a scripture in the Bible that talks about this very thing. It's found in Matthew 5:16, and it says, '*Let your light so shine before men, that they may see your good works, and glorify your Father which is in heaven.*'"

"'*Let your light so shine,*'" Melanie Ann echoed, deep in thought.

"Yes, you have to keep your light shining bright, and that means following God's commands and letting others see—in your words and your actions—that you are a Christian. All the time. No matter what!"

Melanie Ann sighed as she pondered her grandmother's words. "That's not always easy for me, especially when my friends are doing the *wrong* thing and they want me to go along with them. It's so hard, Grand Doll."

"Oh, I know it is," Grand Doll agreed. She then went on to explain, "But one of the ways we let our lights shine is by having a good reputation. My mother used to say, 'Honey, it is not what you do, it is what people *think* you do.' She meant that we all need to guard our hearts and actions. As Christians, we are lights, and there are always people watching what we do. That is why it is always so important to do the right thing."

"Sometimes it's hard to do the right thing," Melanie Ann shrugged.

"Trust me, we all hide our lights sometimes, whether we mean to or not!" her grandmother said. "But that's part of the journey—learning how to let your light shine, even when it's really tough."

Melanie Ann nodded as she looked at the photo of Grand Doll dressed as the Statue of Liberty. She thought about all of her friends at school, the ones who said they loved God but didn't act like it. She didn't want to be like that. She wanted the joy of the Lord to shine through all of the time, even when things weren't going so well.

"I want to be like Lady Liberty!" she whispered. "I want to let my light shine too…for all the world to see!"

With a smile on her face, she turned her attentions back to her grandmother, ready to hear more about Sarah Jane.

"Let your light so shine before men, that they may see your good works, and glorify your Father which is in heaven."

—Matthew 5:16

THE LEGACY OF BEING A GOOD WITNESS

"ARE YOU GETTING HUNGRY?" GRAND Doll asked, closing the photo album.

Melanie Ann looked up at the clock on the wall, stunned to discover how late it was. Was it really almost six o'clock? Had she and her grandmother really been talking all of this time? The sun would be going down soon, and there were so many stories she still wanted to hear!

"I'm starved!" she admitted.

"Well, then I think it's time for some dinner." Grand Doll stood up and put the photo album back into the trunk. "We can always talk more at the dinner table."

At the word *dinner*, Splenda woke up from his nap and started wagging his tail.

Grand Doll laughed. "Looks like we're not the only ones who are hungry!"

Melanie Ann followed her grandmother as they made their way into the kitchen. Splenda jumped up and down, hoping he would get some food too.

"I've got some roast beef cooking," her grandmother said, opening the oven. "And potatoes and carrots. How does that sound?"

"Wonderful!" Melanie Ann's tummy began to rumble. "It smells great!" she said.

As her grandmother began to prepare their plates, Melanie Ann offered to set the table. She loved putting the beautiful plates and napkins in place.

"Thanks, honey," Grand Doll said. "I have a wonderful idea. Let's eat in the big dining room tonight on the white damask tablecloth, with the special dishes—the Castleton Rose china."

"Really? We can use the fine china?" she asked, the excitement obvious in her voice.

"Why not? It will give us the perfect setting for the rest of Sarah Jane's story! We can pretend we live in the 1800s in a fine house in Pennsylvania. How would that be?"

Melanie Ann giggled. "Sounds like a blast. Should we use the crystal goblets too?"

"Of course! The Rose Point crystal stemware would be perfect. Don't forget the lace napkins and the Lily of the Valley silver. After dinner, we'll have tea in the demitasse teacups, along with your favorite—German chocolate cake!"

"Mmm!"

Melanie Ann quickly made her way to the elegant dining room and began setting the table for dinner. She grew even more excited when she saw the white candles on the table and the beautiful white floral centerpiece. As she laid out the china and goblets, she thought about all of the girls in her family—not just the ones from the past, but the ones from the present too. She had so many cousins who were girls…and a younger sister also. Would they grow up to be like the girls in the stories? Would they learn to let their lights shine like Sarah Jane? Would they leave a legacy?

A few minutes later, Grand Doll joined her at the table. After they had held hands and prayed over their food, it was time to eat. Melanie Ann put her cloth napkin in her lap and smiled at her grandmother. What a wonderful time they were having together, acting like royalty! How special to have Grand Doll all to herself.

They started with a salad of mixed greens and then enjoyed a delicious bowl of soup. Melanie Ann loved having her meal in different courses! Next, it was time for the hot food. Roast beef was her favorite. But then, of course, Grand Doll knew that. By making everything seem so special, she always made everyone *feel* special.

"Would you please pass the salt and pepper, Grand Doll?" Melanie Ann asked in her most prim and proper voice.

"Certainly, Miss Henderson!"

Melanie Ann giggled when Grand Doll called her by her last name. Then, being as ladylike as she could, she took a nibble of the roast beef. All the while, she thought of Sarah Jane. How hard it would be to *always* act like a lady! Sometimes it was fun to pretend, but to be ladylike *all* the time would be another thing altogether!

Careful not to make a mess, Melanie Ann dabbed her lips with the napkin in between bites. She tried not to giggle. "Was there something more you wanted to tell me about the Statue of Liberty, Grand Doll?" she asked at last.

"Hmm." Her grandmother was silent for a moment as she thought about it. "I know that people came to New York Harbor in ships from other countries. The first thing they saw when they sailed into the harbor was Lady Liberty, with her torch shining bright. She welcomed them there."

"Why did so many people come to America?" Melanie Ann asked.

"Many came searching for the American dream. They were willing to work hard and were determined to find a better life," replied Grand Doll.

Pretending to hold a torch, Melanie Ann lifted up the salt shaker and smiled broadly.

A serious look passed over her grandmother's face as she began to explain to Melanie Ann, "See, honey, I want to leave behind a legacy of being a good witness. I want to let my light shine."

"Oh, you do, Grand Doll," Melanie Ann said. "You're always telling others about Jesus."

"Yes, but there's more to my plan," her grandmother said. "I want to teach my children and my grandchildren to do the same. I want everyone in my family to understand just how important it is to let his or her light shine. That scripture tells us to, '*Let your light so shine before men, that they may see your good works, and glorify your Father which is in heaven.*' Would you like to know why?"

"Why?" Melanie Ann asked, taking another bite of the delicious food.

"Because there are so many people in the world who don't yet know the Lord. If we let our lights shine, people will wonder what makes us different. When they ask, we can say, 'It's the love of God shining in our eyes!'"

"I see," Melanie Ann said with a nod. She wanted people to see the love of God shining in her eyes, for sure!

"Have you ever heard of the Great Commission?" Grand Doll asked.

"Yes, I learned that scripture verse from the book of Matthew when I was little," Melanie Ann responded. "It says we're supposed to go into all the world and preach the Gospel so that others can come to know the Lord." She put her fork down, ready to ask a question. "I've always wondered about that. How can I go into all the world? I'm only fourteen. And can anyone really go into the whole world?"

A smile lit up Grand Doll's face. "Well, this is what I think. You are called to bloom where you are planted. In other words, you have a certain group of friends in a certain school, in a certain city, and a certain state. That's your own little world. Imagine how many people you could reach—in your school, your city, and your state—if you would keep your light shining brightly. Your entire little world would be reached."

"Oh, I see!"

"Now think about Christians all over the big, wide world. If they would all keep their lights shining brightly, people in their countries, their communities, and their families could come to know Christ. Before long, hundreds, maybe even thousands, of people would come to know Him—if they just kept their torches lit like Lady Liberty."

"I think I understand," Melanie Ann said, taking a bite of a potato. "God isn't expecting just one or two people to do the work. If we *all* let our lights shine, then we can all play a role. Is that right?"

"Yes!" Her grandmother's face lit into a smile. "And that is a legacy I want to pass down to you grandchildren. I want you to know how very important it is to me—and how important it was to others such as my parents and grandparents—that my children and grandchildren carry on the legacy of being a good witness."

"I'll do my best, I promise!"

Grand Doll stood to go back into the kitchen, and then she returned a few moments later with the beautiful German chocolate cake in her hands.

"Mmm. That looks great!" Melanie Ann said.

"Indeed it does! I promised you an exciting weekend, with stories and a special luxury suite in which to sleep. What good would any of that be if we didn't get to celebrate over a wonderful meal and have your favorite dessert! Don't you see, Melanie Ann? I want this to be a weekend you will never forget. Years from now, I want you to be able to tell your children about this night. So have a piece of cake. It will be the perfect ending to an already exciting day."

Melanie Ann giggled as she cut off a large slice. If eating a slice of German chocolate cake could somehow help her be a good witness, she would gladly eat it. In fact, she might eat two!

"I believe in the legacy of hard work," her grandmother said. "That's something I want to pass on to you children as well."

THE DUTCH
DOLL QUILT

*A*FTER EATING A LARGE SLICE OF CAKE, Melanie Ann helped Grand Doll with the dishes. Afterward, she brushed her teeth and changed into her pajamas, then went into the luxury suite, as her grandmother called it. She hoped there would be time for one more story before climbing into bed.

Just then, Grand Doll appeared at the bedroom door, dressed in her pink satin robe and fuzzy slippers. A broad smile lit her face, and her cheeks glowed with excitement. "Before you go to sleep, I wanted to let you know that I'm so happy you're here with me. I'm having such a wonderful time."

"Oh, me too!" Melanie Ann agreed. In fact, she couldn't remember when she'd ever had more fun at her grandmother's house. She couldn't wait to tell her brother, sister, and cousins about all that she had learned. What would they think about all of the little women in Grand Doll's stories?

"Aren't you glad you're the oldest of the grandchildren?" her grandmother asked.

"I am." She didn't know when she'd ever been happier about that.

"I'll share more stories in the morning," Grand Doll said with a nod.

Melanie Ann's heart raced with excitement. "I'm sure they're going to be great!"

"Oh, they are!" Her grandmother helped her turn down the covers on the tall four-poster bed. They pushed the big throw pillows out of the way, and Melanie Ann climbed up, up, up, until finally snuggling under the warmth of the fancy covers.

Grand Doll took a seat on the edge of the bed and reached to take her hand. "I'm so excited about tomorrow! That's when I'll give you the key to the trunk."

"I can't wait!" Melanie Ann said. "And I promise to keep it in a safe place."

"Would you like to hear one more story before you go to sleep?" Grand Doll asked. "Or are you too tired?"

"I was hoping there would be time for another. And I'm never too tired for a story!" Melanie Ann leaned back against the pillows, ready to hear what her grandmother would say next.

Grand Doll pointed to a brass quilt rack on the far side of the room. "Do you see that pretty Dutch doll quilt?" she asked.

Melanie Ann gave it a quick glance, noticing the beautiful colors. "Oh, is that what you call it?"

"Yes, my mother made that quilt when I was a little girl. I can remember seeing it hanging on the clothesline, drying in the sunshine. When I got married, my mother passed it down to me. One of these days when you're all grown up, perhaps it will be in your home."

"Really?" Melanie Ann gazed at it more carefully this time. Amazed at its beautiful hand-stitching, she wondered what the quilt must have looked like hanging on a clothesline in the afternoon sun.

"Yes, it's one of my most prized possessions. That's why I haven't put it into the trunk yet. I want to keep it on display for everyone to see. It reminds me of my childhood every time I look at it."

Just then, something occurred to Melanie Ann. "You know, Grand Doll," she said at last, "you've told me a lot about the girls in our family, but I don't know anything about what you were like as a girl. I'll bet you have some great stories!"

Her grandmother smiled. "I grew up during the Great Depression and World War II. I lived on a dairy farm just a few miles from here in Mexia, Texas."

"I remember learning about the Great Depression in school," Melanie Ann said. "Lots of people were out of work, and some even went without food."

"Yes, it was quite a difficult time in our country's history," Grand Doll said. "People had to work really hard just to get by, but my parents knew how to make hard work fun." She walked toward the Dutch doll quilt, which she removed from the rack and carried over to the bed. "Do you see these tiny stitches?" she asked, pointing to the lovely quilt.

Melanie Ann squinted to see. Sure enough, there were little bitty stitches all over the quilt. They were hardly visible from a distance, but up close, she could see them plainly.

"My mother made every one of these delicate stitches by hand, with a quilting needle and thread. She worked for weeks and weeks to make this quilt."

"Wow. Seems like a lot of work for one quilt. Why didn't she just go to the store and buy one?"

Grand Doll smiled. "Well, that's not how they did it back then, especially during the Great Depression. People made most everything from scratch. My mother made most of our clothes and even had our shoes resoled. She also grew most of our vegetables in her garden and canned them for the wintertime. My papa raised hogs and chickens, so we always had plenty to eat. And there was always milk to drink, because we had dairy cows."

"Did you milk the cows?" Melanie Ann asked.

"I tried a time or two, but Papa was better at it than I was, to be sure!"

Something about this just didn't make sense. "Didn't they have grocery stores back then?" Melanie Ann asked.

"In some cities, yes, but people simply didn't spend money on things they could make or grow themselves. They worked hard for everything."

Melanie Ann thought about how tough it would be if they couldn't go to the grocery store to purchase the things they needed. Why, they bought all of their food there—bread, milk, ice cream—everything! What if she had to grow vegetables in a garden? Could she do it? And how would they get meat to eat and juice to drink?

"My parents both worked really hard at everything they did," Grand Doll continued. "And my mother knew how to turn work into a game, so I grew up having a lot of fun while doing chores around the farm, folding laundry, and tidying up my room."

"Wow," Melanie Ann responded, shaking her head. She simply couldn't imagine it. "Cleaning my room is *no* fun."

Grand Doll laughed long and hard at that one. "Oh, trust me…my mama could make anything fun, even the difficult things. I learned to work very hard when I was a little girl."

"And you still do," Melanie Ann said in awe. She knew that her grandmother had accomplished many great things, even running her own business.

"I believe in the legacy of hard work," her grandmother said. "That's something I want to pass on to you children as well. We had a family motto about hard work. It was a scripture found in 2 Chronicles 15:7 that says, *Be ye strong therefore, and let not your hands be weak: for your work shall be rewarded.*"

"I like that," Melanie Ann replied.

"Oh, I can tell you many stories about the value of hard work."

"Mmm-hmm." Melanie Ann couldn't help but let out a yawn, and her grandmother chuckled.

"Okay, sleepyhead, right now I think it's time for bed," Grand Doll said. "There will be plenty of time in the morning to talk about work." She turned off the lamp on the bedside table and leaned over to kiss Melanie Ann on the forehead. "Good night, sweetheart."

"Good night, Grand Doll," Melanie Ann said, stifling another yawn. She rolled over in the bed and pulled the covers over her shoulders. Before long, she was fast asleep, dreaming of covered wagons, sailing ships…and little Dutch dolls dancing on quilts.

Be ye strong therefore, and let not your hands be weak: for your work shall be rewarded.

—2 Chronicles 15:7

THE LEGACY OF
HARD WORK

MELANIE ANN AWOKE TO THE MOST wonderful smell. Was that bacon? She didn't have long to think about it before Splenda jumped onto her bed and licked her on the cheek. Melanie Ann couldn't help but giggle, because it tickled! "You silly dog," she said, as she scratched him behind the ears. He wagged his tail and snuggled up against her, hoping to have his tummy rubbed. She did so, smiling all the while.

After spending a little more time with the dog, Melanie Ann scrambled out of the bed and made her way into the living room, still in her pajamas. There, she found Grand Doll sitting in one of the big leather chairs, drinking Chai tea and reading her Bible.

"Well, good morning, sleepyhead!" her grandmother said.

"Good morning," Melanie Ann said, and she gave Grand Doll a warm hug.

"Did you sleep well in the luxury suite?"

"Oh yes! That bed is soft as feathers, and the comforter is so warm and cozy!"

"Good. Are you hungry? I made pancakes, bacon, and scrambled eggs. How does that sound?"

Melanie Ann's mouth began to water. "Sounds amazing. I think the wonderful smell of bacon woke me up." She usually ate cold cereal for breakfast, so hot breakfast foods sounded like a feast!

Minutes later they were seated at the breakfast table, and Grand Doll prayed over the food. Then it was time to eat. Melanie Ann could hardly wait to taste the fluffy, buttery pancakes and crisp pieces of yummy bacon. The scrambled eggs looked like golden mounds of snow piled up on her plate and were sure to be delicious.

Melanie Ann smothered her pancakes with thick maple syrup and dove in. Every bite tasted wonderful. So did the milk, which sat in a glass to the right of the plate. She took sips in between bites.

"I take it you like the food," Grand Doll commented with a smile.

"You're the best cook in the world," Melanie Ann said, wiping a bit of syrup from her chin with a napkin. "Thank you for going to so much trouble for me."

"Why, you're welcome, honey. It was no trouble at all. I'm used to working hard! It's a pleasure to have someone to cook for!"

Melanie Ann paused and looked into her grandmother's beautiful brown eyes. What fun this weekend was turning out to be!

Grand Doll interrupted her thoughts. "Eating breakfast with you reminds me of when I was a girl," she said with a twinkle in her eye.

"Really? Why is that?"

"Well, this morning I made these pancakes from scratch—I didn't use a box mix. That's just how my mama used to make them too. She mixed up the flour, the eggs, the butter, and the other ingredients. Pancakes are so much better homemade."

"They are great!" In fact, Melanie Ann didn't know when she'd ever had better pancakes.

"I purchased the eggs at the grocery store," Grand Doll observed. "Same with the bacon. But my mama never would have done that. Certainly not!"

"Really? How come?" Melanie Ann asked. "Eggs didn't come from a store when you were little?"

Her grandmother chuckled. "There were no grocery stores where I lived—not during the Great Depression, anyway. We had hens, and they were kept in a henhouse. It was my job to collect the eggs once a day. My mama would fry them or scramble them. And, of course, she used them to bake with. And the bacon…well, let's just say, Papa certainly knew how to butcher a hog."

Melanie Ann gasped. "Oh, Grand Doll, really?"

Her grandmother smiled. "Yes. Remember, we lived on a dairy farm. We had lots of animals. The milk I drank came from our own cows."

"Did it taste like this milk?" Melanie Ann asked.

"Oh, it was even better!" Grand Doll grinned and then began to describe the creamy taste of the milk she used to drink.

"Still, before you could eat breakfast, someone had to do chores like milking the cows and gathering the eggs?" Melanie Ann asked thoughtfully.

"Yes, that's right. And then it all had to be cooked."

"It sounds like a lot of work just for one meal," Melanie Ann admitted. "I'm getting tired just thinking about it. By the time you finished doing all of those things, you were probably too tired to eat!"

"It was tiring, but we didn't mind—and I was certainly never too tired to eat," Grand Doll said. "As I mentioned last night, my mama—your great-grandmother—really knew how to make hard work fun. And that's the legacy I mentioned that I hope to leave behind to you. Remember the scripture I told you last night? About your hard work being rewarded?"

"Can you tell me again?"

"*Be ye strong therefore, and let not your hands be weak: for your work shall be rewarded.*"

Melanie Ann thought about that a moment. "I don't mind hard work...although I hope I never have to butcher a hog!" she added with a giggle.

"Surely not," her grandmother added with a laugh. "But you do have to work hard, don't you? You go to school, do your homework, help your mother around the house, play ball, and do your chores."

"And I help out at church too. Once a month, I work in the children's ministry," she explained. "I like to stay busy, and I especially love caring for the children."

"You're more like me than you know then!" Grand Doll said. "The Great Depression wasn't the only obstacle we faced when I was a little girl. Just a few years after the Depression ended, our country went through World War II. Our young men in the armed services needed our help, so many of us children back at home formed what were called Victory Clubs. I was the leader of our local Victory Club in Mexia, and it was quite a job, let me tell you!"

"Victory Club? What was that?" asked Melanie Ann.

"Well, during the war, there were many things that had to be done. While the soldiers were overseas fighting, the people back home had to do their part. It was called the 'war effort.' We had to ration food and clothes, collect scrap metal for the military, and do all sorts of other things. I remember wanting to do my part as well. That is why I helped form the Victory Club. All of us girls at school got together and started helping with the war effort. We wrote letters to the soldiers and collected money for the American Red Cross. Probably my favorite part was planting a Victory flower garden. We grew flowers and gave them to the families of those who were serving in the military. I will never forget the faces of the dear mothers who had boys or husbands fighting in the war. Thinking of them still brings tears to my eyes."

"Wow, Grand Doll, even back then you were doing things for others," said Melanie Ann.

"Staying busy is a blessing. There's something wonderful about good, hard work. My papa always used to say, 'When the going gets tough, the tough get going.'"

Melanie Ann laughed. "I must be tough then, because I like to keep going." She paused for a moment, then looked at her grandmother. "I think all of the girls in our family must have been hard workers."

"Oh yes," Grand Doll said. "And if I know you, you're going to be just like them. I predict that you will go on working hard when you're a grown woman too!"

"I'm sure you're right."

As they finished up their meal, Melanie Ann offered to help with the dishes. She and her grandmother had great fun as they rinsed the plates and put them in the dishwasher.

"We didn't have one of these when I was a little girl," her grandmother said, pointing to the dishwasher. "In fact, we washed every dish by hand. Then we dried them with dishcloths and put them away."

"So the work never ended?" Melanie Ann asked.

"That's right. It never ended," Grand Doll replied, grinning. "But that's how life is in general—the work never ends. When you're young, you work hard in school. When you're grown, you work hard in college. After that, you get a good job and work hard at it. Then you get married and have children…and trust me, children are the most work of all!"

They both laughed together before Grand Doll announced it was time to go back into the living room for more stories. Melanie Ann dried her hands on a dishtowel, and then, with Splenda following along behind her, she returned with her grandmother to the old black trunk, curious to see what adventures lay ahead.

"Next to your relationship with the Lord, the people in your family are the most special of all."

Eleven

As for Me and My House

ONCE THEY HAD ARRIVED BACK IN THE living room, Grand Doll went to her recliner and picked up the worn leather Bible she'd been reading earlier. As she held it tightly in her hand, tears came to her eyes, and Melanie Ann wondered why.

"This was my mother's Bible," her grandmother said finally, as she dabbed at her eyes. "Of all the many Bibles I own, this one is my very favorite."

"Really?"

"Yes. Do you see how the leather has grown soft?" She placed it into Melanie Ann's outstretched hands.

"Yes, it's very soft," Melanie Ann replied, nodding. She carefully ran her fingertips across the cover.

"That's because my mama used it every day for years and years. She depended on this Bible to see her through the hard times."

"Wow. So this is the Bible she read when your family was going through the Great Depression and World War II?" Melanie Ann asked, holding it a bit tighter.

"Oh yes, she read it every morning. It brought her great joy and comfort. Most nights, we would gather together in the living room, and then my papa would read to us children from this Bible." Grand Doll took the Bible once again and looked at it lovingly. She pointed to several names that Melanie Ann recognized—her aunts, uncles, parents, grandparents, and great-grandparents.

"These are the names of many of your relatives," her grandmother explained. "Some you know, and others you do not."

"Yes, I do recognize many of the names," Melanie Ann said, looking again.

"Now I want to talk with you for a minute about the importance of family," her grandmother said with a serious look on her face. "Next to your relationship with the Lord, the people in your family are the most special of all."

Melanie Ann's heart grew happy as she thought about her grandmother's wise words. She loved her parents and her brother and sister. She also loved her grandparents and cousins.

"I remember so many things about my childhood," Grand Doll said with a smile. "I could tell you all about the dairy farm where I grew up, the small town I lived in, the friends I met in school…but the very best memories of all are about my family." Her eyes began to twinkle as she added, "Would you like to hear a wonderful family-related story from my childhood?"

"Oh yes!" Melanie Ann said.

"This is a Christmas story," Grand Doll said with a nod. "One year when I was very young, our family had no money to buy Christmas presents. It was during the Great Depression."

"No money at all?" Melanie Ann could hardly imagine such a thing.

"Well, my parents had saved up two dollars," Grand Doll explained, "but that wasn't enough to buy gifts for all of us children."

"Two dollars?" Melanie Ann was absolutely astounded at this news. Why, two dollars was hardly enough to buy a loaf of bread these days, let alone Christmas presents! "What did your mother and father do?" she asked nervously.

Grand Doll's face lit up as she told the rest of the story. "They used the money for gas, and we drove to Dallas to look at the Christmas windows."

"Christmas windows?"

"Yes, back in those days, big department stores had beautiful Christmas displays in the windows. There were snowmen and elves, Santa and his reindeer—oh, the things I saw that day! What a wonderful memory it is."

Grand Doll's smile widened a bit as she added, "But the best part was what happened when we got home."

"What happened?" Melanie Ann asked.

"It was a miracle, really," Grand Doll explained. "Someone had come into our house while we were gone."

"Someone broke into your house?" Melanie Ann asked, shocked that her grandmother would be happy about such a thing.

"Well, not exactly," Grand Doll said with a chuckle. "Not like you're thinking, anyway. They came inside and left lots and lots of presents under the tree for us!"

"Wow!"

"Oh my, yes. There were lovely things under that tree—for all of us. There were clothes, toys, a doll, and even a little china tea set."

"That's amazing!" Melanie Ann said in awe.

"And that's not all," Grand Doll said. "The kitchen table was loaded with food. We had everything you could ever want for a Christmas dinner, and more!"

"Did you ever find out who did it?" Melanie Ann asked.

"We never did," Grand Doll replied, "though I think my parents had their suspicions. But I can tell you without a doubt that it was the most delightful Christmas of my life—not just because of the gifts and the food, but because my parents cared enough to drive us all the way to Dallas to see those Christmas windows. Oh, what wonderful memories I have of that experience." She gave Melanie Ann a pat on the shoulder. "And you know just how that feels, don't you? Some of your best memories are about your family too."

Melanie Ann had to agree. Her *very* best memories were about her family.

"My parents were wonderful people," Grand Doll continued. "When I think about my mama, I am so thankful for what a wonderful woman of God she was and that she gave me a Christian heritage. Her love was unconditional and sacrificial. She never went to bed at night until the house was straight, clean, and all housework completed. Mama never raised her voice. I never heard her talk badly about anyone. I never heard of any of her family *ever* fussing. They were always kind to each other and loving to everyone. Mama displayed all of the fruits of the Spirit through her actions. Not only did my mother know how to make work fun, she also knew how to show love to us children."

Melanie Ann sighed, wishing she could have known her great-grandmother who was affectionately called "Bobo." She sounded so wonderful. "I hope I can be a mother like that one day," she said.

"Keep walking with the Lord, and you will!" her grandmother said. She sighed deeply. "Now, let me tell you about my papa. He was the greatest man I ever knew."

"Wow." He must've been pretty special for Grand Doll to get that dreamy-eyed look!

"My relationship with my earthly father taught me so much about my heavenly Father," Grand Doll explained. "Nothing can change the love of God, just like nothing could change the love of my father. Like God, my father's love was unconditional and sacrificial."

"Sacrificial?"

"Yes. He would have done anything for his family. He worked day and night. He protected me and provided for all of my needs and most of my wants. My father was such a godly man."

"He sounds like an amazing father—like mine," Melanie Ann agreed.

"Yes, he was wonderful. Both my parents were. I loved them so very much, and I never wanted to hurt them in any way. They taught me how to be a good parent myself. I can't even begin to tell you how much I love all of my children and grandchildren. And your Poppie…," she said, her eyes growing misty. "I miss your grandfather so much now that he's living in a nursing home, but I still love him as much as the day I married him."

"Oh, Grand Doll, I miss him too." Melanie Ann reached over to give her grandmother a hug.

"I am a blessed woman to have such wonderful people in my life."

"Me too," Melanie Ann whispered, suddenly realizing just how blessed she was.

"You see, honey," her grandmother said, "there is no greater earthly gift in the world than the gift of family. God has given you parents, a brother, a sister, grandparents, cousins, and other relatives…as a gift."

"Wow, I never thought about my family as a gift before," Melanie Ann said.

"Oh yes," Grand Doll said, nodding. "Family members are like presents you unwrap, one at a time. They're all different, but they are all priceless. Of course, the very best kind of family is one that serves the Lord."

"That reminds me of a verse I read in the Bible," Melanie Ann said. "I think it's in the book of Joshua, in the Old Testament. May I borrow your Bible to look it up?"

"Of course!"

Melanie Ann took the worn leather Bible in her hands and opened it to the book of Joshua, chapter 24. She smiled as she read verse 15: "*But as for me and my house…*"

"*We will serve the LORD!*" Grand Doll finished the last part with her.

"Yes," Melanie Ann said with a grin. "*But as for me and my house, we will serve the LORD.*"

"That means everyone in the house," her grand-mother explained, "which is why it is so important to keep praying for the ones who don't know the Lord yet."

"Yes." Melanie Ann couldn't help but smile. "I'm so glad the people in our family are Christians—that they love the Lord."

"It hasn't always been that way," Grand Doll said. "There was a time when your Aunt Sherrie wasn't walking with the Lord."

"Really?"

"Yes," Grand Doll replied, nodding. "I prayed and fasted for several days, never giving up, just like the verse from Joshua says we should do. I kept praying and believing, even when things didn't look good."

"What happened?"

Her grandmother smiled. "After about three weeks, Sherrie came to me and told me the most remarkable story of how she had finally given her heart to the Lord. And you know, Melanie Ann, your Aunt Sherrie has now served the Lord for many, many years. Why, she's even done missionary work in foreign lands."

"What a great story!" Melanie Ann agreed. "I'm so glad you didn't stop praying!"

"That reminds me of an expression I used to hear when I was little," her grandmother said.

"What's that?"

"'The family that prays together stays together.' Have you ever heard that saying?"

"Hmm. I don't think so." It didn't sound familiar to Melanie Ann at all.

"I've heard it all my life," her grandmother said with a smile, "and it's so true. If you want to have a really strong family, then it's important for every member to have a strong faith. And those are the legacies I hope to leave behind when I'm gone—family, faith, and love. It's hard to have one without the other! That's why this Bible means so much to me. It represents the faith of my parents and grandparents."

"And *your* faith too," Melanie Ann added. Everyone knew that Grand Doll loved the Lord. She talked about her great faith in the Lord all the time and encouraged others to do the same.

"And yours too," her grandmother said. "One day this Bible will be yours, and you will be able to share with your children the importance of faith in God." She turned back to the front of the Bible, pointing again to the names written there.

"Take a close look at this, Melanie Ann. It's our family tree."

"What's a family tree?" she asked, curious to learn about the interesting-looking diagram.

Her grandmother smiled. "It's called a family tree because you start at the top by writing your name. Under that, you put the names of your parents. Under that, you put the names of their parents, and so forth. By the time you're finished, it takes the shape of a tree!"

"I see," Melanie Ann said. It sounded like a lot of fun.

"When we are finished looking through the trunk, I'll help you build your family tree," Grand Doll said. "How does that sound?"

"Sounds great! Do you know all of the names?" Melanie Ann asked.

"I know most of them," her grandmother said. "Maybe we can search the Internet to find the rest. I think you will be surprised to see just how big our tree is!"

Melanie Ann giggled as she thought about everything her grandmother had said. From all the stories she'd heard, her family tree must be the biggest in the world!

But as for me and my house,
we will serve the Lord.

—Joshua 24:15

THE LEGACY
OF FAMILY

*L*ET'S TALK A BIT MORE ABOUT THE LEGACY of family," Grand Doll said with a happy look on her face. "Come into the sunroom with me, and we will look at a few photographs. I think you will enjoy them. I know I do."

Melanie Ann followed behind her grandmother as they made their way into the room Grand Doll liked to call the "Son" room—the glassed-in room at the back of the house where she often read her Bible and prayed. The late morning sunlight streamed through the window, and the green plants inside the room seemed to glow.

Once inside, Melanie Ann took a seat on the white wicker sofa. Splenda curled up at her feet, letting out a yawn. What a perfect place to sit and rest…and drink tea! Melanie Ann could imagine sitting here every morning, watching the sun come up. Perhaps that's what Grand Doll did.

She watched her grandmother pick up a large photo album with tattered edges, opening it to the first page. Grand Doll smiled as she pointed to a photograph of a family seated together on the front porch of a house. It was an old black-and-white picture, and a little faded, at that. Melanie Ann gave it a curious look.

The woman on the left wore a white dress with a high collar and sat straight as an arrow, her dark hair swept back behind her ear. The little girl on the middle step was cute as a button. The boy at the bottom of the photo looked to be quite young and had mischief in his big brown eyes. He wore striped overalls over a white, collared shirt. The father in the picture leaned his elbows against his knees, and gazed out, as if wondering who might one day be looking at the photo. Did he know that Melanie Ann was looking, even now?

The girl in the center of the picture—the one with the flowered dress and the white Peter Pan collar—looked a lot like…

Melanie Ann looked up at her grandmother with curiosity. Yes, the girl looked a lot like Grand Doll!

"Is that you?" Melanie Ann asked, amazed.

"Oh yes," Grand Doll said with a smile. "That photo was taken when I was just nine years old. There's my mama," she said, pointing to the woman in the white dress. "And my papa. And my little brother and sister."

"Wow." They looked just as Melanie Ann had pictured.

Her grandmother nodded. "That was a very special day for our family. You see, back in those days, photographs were rare. So it was a privilege to have our picture taken."

That was hard for Melanie Ann to imagine. She used her digital camera to take photos all the time, even uploading most of them to the computer for her friends to see. Why, she could even take pictures on her cell phone and send them to others in no time at all. How sad not to be able to take lots and lots of pictures of those you loved!

Grand Doll's eyes grew misty as she stared at the photograph. "I remember this day so well. I had left my reader *See Spot Run* at home, so my mother walked over a mile to the schoolhouse to bring it to me. We were having our pictures taken in school that day, and when my mother saw the photographer there, she decided it would also be a great day to have a family picture taken. So she asked a friend who owned a red box camera to take the picture, and after school, our whole family gathered together on the porch to capture the memory of that day."

Melanie Ann looked at the photograph a little more carefully this time. "Sounds like your mom had a really great idea!"

"Oh, she did," Grand Doll said. "The reason I remember the day so well is that she took the time to get it all on film. I will never forget how she loved me enough to walk all that way to bring my little reader to school. But you know what I remember most of all?"

"What?"

"How much I loved all of the people *in* the picture. And I'm so glad the moment was captured on film. See, honey, that's what I want to talk to you about…"

"What do you mean?"

"I want to encourage you to create memories with your family. Capture every little thing. Be a memory maker."

"A memory maker? How do I do that?"

"There are several things you can do," Grand Doll explained. "Keeping photo albums and scrapbooks is one thing. Take photos as often as you can—at family gatherings, vacations, birthday parties, and other times when you're all together."

"I love taking pictures," Melanie Ann said.

"Great! Then become your family's official photographer! You can also do scrap-booking. Put your photos in an album. Add colorful bits of paper and trim, and write down funny captions under each photo. I like to call them memory books. You will have a wonderful time making memories!" Grand Doll said with a wink. "Another great thing you can do is to write down your family's traditions in a journal."

"Like how we celebrate holidays and birthdays?"

"Yes," Grand Doll said, "and you can write about the special places you've gone together, the vacations you've taken, or the games you like to play. Why, you can even write down the goofy jokes you tell and the kinds of foods you like to eat or the special recipes you make. Write it all down so that your children will know about you and your family. You could even save your memories on your computer, burn them onto CDs, and then place them in a safe where they will be kept forever."

"Sounds great!" Melanie Ann said.

"I'm glad you think so," Grand Doll replied. "One of these days when you're my age, you will enjoy looking through photo albums and reading journals. It will mean so much to you and to others in the family."

"You always have the best ideas," Melanie Ann asserted. "I hope I'm just like you when I'm grown."

"Thank you, honey. That means a lot to me. But the person I really want you to be like is Jesus." Grand Doll paused a moment, then added something else. "You know, I've told you how much our family means to me, but I don't think I've told you just how important families are to God."

"To God?"

"Yes. He came up with the idea for families in the first place. Remember, God created Adam and Eve! They had children, and then their children had children. The story went on and on. There have been families ever since."

"I never thought about that before, but I guess you're right," Melanie Ann said.

"Of course! And think about this—the Lord deliberately placed you in *our* family for a reason. Did you ever think about the fact that He specifically chose your parents and the rest of your relatives?"

"Wow."

"Yes. He knew exactly the right family for you. He didn't place you with the family next door or a family on the other side of the world. He picked just the right family for you."

"That's neat to think about, Grand Doll."

"Yes, and think about this—if people didn't get married and have children, there would be no future generations. God knew what He was doing when He created mothers and fathers. They play a very special role. And your parents chose to raise you to serve God. They honored the scripture that says, *But as for me and my house, we will serve the LORD.*"

A smile crossed Melanie Ann's face as she thought about that.

"Your parents have been given quite a task—to raise you and your brother and sister to love the Lord and to teach you to worship God. The family is also the best place to discover your gifts and abilities."

"Like playing ball?" Melanie Ann asked.

"Yes, in your case, playing softball. And taking care of the sick, of course. But think of all the children with different sorts of gifts such as playing an instrument, singing, or creating artwork. Wise parents will help their children discover their gifts and develop them. Then the children can use their gifts to minister to others."

"Wow." Melanie Ann shook her head. "Sounds like being a parent is a lot of work."

"Oh, it's hard work, all right," Grand Doll agreed. "But the best work in the world is the kind a mother or a father does in caring for children. Children are a heritage from the Lord…that's what the Bible says."

"What does that mean?"

"It means *you* are my legacy," her grandmother whispered, slipping an arm around Melanie Ann's shoulders. "You are my gift, my inheritance, and I treasure you more than any of those items we found in the big black trunk."

Melanie Ann couldn't help but smile at that. She made a decision right then and there to capture as many memories as she could. And she would hold them near her heart…for the rest of her life.

And now abide faith, hope, love, these three; but the greatest of these is love.

—1 Corinthians 13:13 NKJV

THE GREATEST OF
THESE IS LOVE

W E'RE NEARLY DONE WITH OUR
stories," Grand Doll said at last.
"Only one more to go, but it's the
most wonderful of all!"

Melanie Ann stared down into the big black trunk,
amazed at all of the items inside. She didn't want to see
this adventure come to an end. She was having such a
great time with her grandmother, and she had learned so
much already. Surely she could sit all day and hear story
after story!

Grand Doll stood and walked to the far end of the
living room, where she pointed to a lighted, life-size
picture that hung on the wall over an old mahogany table.
The picture was a beautiful portrait of Jesus in an ornate
gold frame. The picture's colors were truly amazing, for
the light shining from Jesus' eyes seemed to radiate love.

"This is my most prized possession," she whispered,
touching it with care. "It belonged to my mother. Do you

see the light behind the portrait—how it makes Jesus' eyes shine?"

"Yes." Melanie Ann had seen the picture many times, and had always loved it. There was something rather touching about the glow in Jesus' eyes. Oftentimes as a youngster, she had stood and stared into those loving eyes, feeling the presence of God settle over her.

"I've talked to you about so many different things I want to pass down to my children and grandchildren," Grand Doll said at last. "I want each of you to have a love for God, a love for your country, and a love for your family. I want you to work hard and never give up. It's also my prayer that you let your lights shine—that you are good witnesses for Christ. These are all lasting legacies."

"I'll do my best, Grand Doll," Melanie Ann said. "I promise."

"As the keeper of the key, I'm sure you will!" her grandmother said. "But there is one thing left to talk about, and it's the most important legacy of all."

"What is that?"

Grand Doll reached for her Bible and thumbed through it until she found the verse she was looking for, 1 Corinthians 13:13. "*And now abide faith, hope, love, these three;*" she read aloud, "*but the greatest of these is love*" (NKJV).

"Love is the greatest?" Melanie Ann asked, confused. She would have guessed faith was the greatest.

Grand Doll looked up from the Bible with a smile. "Having faith is so important, honey. We wouldn't make it very far without it! And having hope is quite important too. But according to this verse in First Corinthians, love is the most important thing of all."

Melanie Ann thought about the scripture's words for a moment. She couldn't help but wonder what made love the *most* important.

"It was love that caused God to send His Son, Jesus, into the world to save us from our sins," Grand Doll explained. "And it was love that caused Jesus to walk that long road up Calvary to the cross. He didn't have to go, but He chose to go. That's the very definition of love."

"He chose to love us even when we weren't loveable," Melanie Ann whispered.

"Yes, and aren't you glad He did?"

"Very glad!"

Her grandmother nodded. "And there's another verse that backs that up. It's found in John 15:13." She turned in her Bible and began to read, "'*Greater love hath no man than this, that a man lay down his life for his friends.*'" Jesus loved us so much that He laid down his life for us, His friends. He performed the ultimate sacrifice...just for us."

"I've never thought of it that way." Melanie Ann gazed up into the shining eyes in the picture, eyes that seemed to flow with love…for *her*.

"Out of His great love for our family, God has provided for us, year after year, century after century. He traveled with Mary Elizabeth on the *Assurance*. He was right there when her family built their home in Virginia." Grand Doll's voice grew more serious as she spoke. "It was the mighty hand of God that gave Victoria Grace the courage to nurse wounded soldiers back to health during the Revolutionary War. It was the comforting presence of the Lord that caused Katie Sue to trust Him for the changes in her life when her family traveled all the way across the country in a covered wagon to settle in a new place."

"The same God was there throughout our family's history," Melanie Ann said, finally understanding. "No matter where people lived or what they did for a living, He was always there."

"Yes, the people changed. The stories changed. Even the states changed. But God never changed. He chose to walk alongside our family members each step of the way! He was there on the day Sarah Jane first laid eyes on the Statue of Liberty. It was the Lord who whispered in her ear, 'Keep your light shining brightly!'"

Melanie Ann hardly knew what to say, but after a moment something occurred to her. "And it was the Lord who gave your parents the energy to work hard on the farm during the Depression and World War II. It was the Lord who raised *you* up to be a godly mother and grandmother, showing us how to be the best we could be."

"Yes," Grand Doll said with a smile. "And it's the same Lord who works in *your* life every time you call on Him. He's there when you're playing sports. He's there when you close your eyes to sleep at night. He's there when you're facing difficult situations at school. And He will be there when you're grown up with children of your own." She paused for a moment, love streaming from her eyes. "Don't you see, Melanie Ann? God loves us. And because He loves us, He sticks with us. The Bible says in Hebrews 13:5 that He will never leave us or forsake us."

"He loves us." Melanie Ann stared up at the picture once again, captivated by the love of Christ, which seemed to pour down on her. For whatever reason, she felt like crying. "Grand Doll," she said at last, "I don't think I've ever really understood just how much God loves me. But now I get it. I really do. I get it!"

"The love of God goes beyond anything we can understand," her grandmother whispered. "It is truly the greatest gift of all. And, honey, the story of God's great love is truly the greatest story I could ever tell you—far greater than any other you've heard in the past two days." She sighed and then looked at Melanie Ann with a thoughtful gaze. "Remember that story of the two-dollar Christmas that I told you about?"

"Of course!" Why, Melanie Ann didn't think she would forget that amazing story as long as she lived.

"We were given many gifts on that special Christmas," Grand Doll explained, "but I haven't told you about the greatest one of all. That year we had a beautiful snowfall. Everything was white—like sparkling crystals. My papa told me the most wonderful story of God's love. He explained that my heart could be washed as white as that snow on the ground."

"Oh, I know what you're going to say!" Melanie Ann added with a nod. "Your papa must've told you about Jesus."

"That's right. My papa shared the salvation message with me," Grand Doll explained. "He told me that Jesus loved me so much that He died on the cross for me!"

"Oh!" Melanie Ann said with a smile. "I love that story. I asked Jesus into my heart when I was a little girl. I asked Him to forgive me of my sins and to be the Lord of my life."

"Yes, I remember when you did that," Grand Doll said. "On that special day, He washed your sins away and made you white as snow."

At that point, her grandmother began to hum a little song, the same one she had been humming the day before when they opened the trunk for the first time.

"What is that song, Grand Doll?" Melanie Ann asked. "It sounds familiar."

"It's 'I Love to Tell the Story,' one of my favorite hymns."

Melanie Ann giggled. "That song sounds perfect for you! How does it go?"

Grand Doll began to sing in a voice as clear as crystal:

"I love to tell the story of unseen things above,
Of Jesus and His glory, of Jesus and His love.
I love to tell the story, because I know 'tis true;
It satisfies my longings as nothing else can do.
I love to tell the story, 'twill be my theme in glory,
To tell the old, old story of Jesus and His love.

"I love to tell the story; more wonderful it seems
Than all the golden fancies of all our golden dreams.
I love to tell the story, it did so much for me;
And that is just the reason I tell it now to thee.
I love to tell the story, 'twill be my theme in glory,
To tell the old, old story of Jesus and His love.

"I love to tell the story; 'tis pleasant to repeat
What seems, each time I tell it, more wonderfully
sweet.
I love to tell the story, for some have never heard

The message of salvation from God's own holy Word.
I love to tell the story, 'twill be my theme in glory,
To tell the old, old story of Jesus and His love.

"I love to tell the story, for those who know it best
Seem hungering and thirsting to hear it like the rest.
And when, in scenes of glory, I sing the new, new song,
'Twill be the old, old story that I have loved so long.
I love to tell the story, 'twill be my theme in glory,
To tell the old, old story of Jesus and His love."

As the beautiful song rang out, Melanie Ann's eyes grew misty and her heart began to thump loudly. She understood what Grand Doll had been telling her all along. Even though her family stories were wonderful, there was one story greater still—the story of Jesus and His love!

Again, Melanie Ann looked into the soft glow of the eyes in the picture. God loved her, so much so, that He sent His Son Jesus to die on a cross…for *her.* He loved her when she made mistakes. He loved her when she did things right. He loved her, no matter what.

"The love of God is the greatest legacy I can pass on to you, honey," Grand Doll said with tears in her eyes as she finished up the song. "I will give you all sorts of cherished items from this trunk, and you will enjoy looking at them, even telling stories about them. I can even teach you good character traits like honesty and patriotism. But what good would any of those things be without love?"

"'*The greatest of these is love*,'" Melanie Ann whispered.

"Love is the legacy you will pass down to your children," Grand Doll said softly. "When you rock your children in your arms, they will feel it. And when you teach them about Jesus, they will understand the great love He has for them too. Love can solve every problem and right every wrong."

"Solve every problem?"

"That's true. The Bible tells us just how that works in First Corinthians 13:4–8," her grandmother explained. "*Love suffers long and is kind; love does not envy; love does not parade itself, is not puffed up; does not behave rudely, does not seek its own, is not provoked, thinks no evil; does not rejoice in iniquity, but rejoices in the truth; bears all things, believes all things, hopes all things, endures all things. Love never fails*" (NKJV).

"So *that's* what true love is." Melanie Ann stared up into the eyes of Jesus once more as the truth of what she'd learned settled over her. "I will be patient and kind. I won't be jealous or prideful. I won't be rude or think about myself first. I'll forgive others for the wrong things they've done to me." She smiled as she looked over at her grandmother. "I want to be like Jesus."

"Oh, honey, you already are. And that's the reason I wanted you to come here today, don't you see? You are about to become the keeper of the key." Grand Doll rose from her chair and walked to fireplace mantle, where she reached for a small velvet drawstring bag.

Could it be? Was that possibly…the key? Melanie Ann's heart thumped in anticipation.

Grand Doll took a few steps in her direction, then placed the little bag into Melanie Ann's outstretch palm. "The key to the family trunk is now yours," she whispered with tears rolling down her cheeks. She pulled the small iron key out of the bag, and Melanie Ann stared at it in awe.

"It's hard to imagine Mary Elizabeth once held this very key in her hand," she whispered.

"So did Victoria Grace and all of the other girls we've talked about," Grand Doll reminded her.

Melanie Ann held it tightly, thinking about all of those wonderful little women from her grandmother's stories, and then carefully placed the key back into the little velvet bag. Her grandmother gave her a smile.

"This is not the only 'key' I'm going to give to you today."

"It isn't?" Melanie Ann clutched the bag in her hand, curious about her grandmother's words.

"The real key to a successful legacy is love. Always remember the difference. One is a key you can see with your own eyes." Grand Doll pointed to the tiny velvet bag. "The other is a key you must learn to use every day, whether you see it or not, for it is the key that will open the most doors. It is your true legacy."

"I get it, Grand Doll! I get it! Our family has a legacy of love!"

"That's right—the most amazing legacy of all, and one I'm sure you will pass down to the next generation."

"Oh, Grand Doll!" As Melanie Ann spoke, a lump grew up in her throat, and she found it difficult to say the rest. "I *will*. I promise!"

Splenda began to jump up and down, trying to snatch the little velvet bag from Melanie Ann's hand. She quickly put it in her backpack to keep it safe. Once she arrived home, she would put it in her jewelry box, the safest place of all. But for now, she couldn't wait to get back to her grandmother, to spend the rest of the day building their family tree and talking about all of the adventures ahead!

As Melanie Ann turned back to look at Grand Doll, with her white curls and broad smile, a warm feeling passed over the fourteen-year-old. She had learned *so* much about her family, her legacy, and her faith from this amazing woman. Melanie Ann looked into her grandmother's shining brown eyes, beaming with love, and she realized the truth of it. Her grandmother's eyes looked *just* like the eyes of Jesus in the picture above.

They seemed to shine with love—not just for her but for everyone!

Yes, love surely was the key Grand Doll had been talking about all along. And Melanie Ann decided right then and there *she* would be the keeper of that key...for the rest of her life.

Fun Facts and More

§ In the 1600s and 1700s, people came to America from all over the world. Many (like Mary Elizabeth) came on ships like the *Assurance*, to escape religious persecution.

§ There were not always fifty states like there are now. Early in America's history, there were only thirteen colonies, and they were all in the Northeast. All thirteen eventually became states.

§ A *patriot* is "someone who loves and/or defends his or her country." Revolutionary patriots (like Victoria Grace) loved their country and wanted to be free from British rule so that they could govern themselves.

§ During the mid to late 1800s, thousands of Americans (like Katie Sue) traveled west in covered wagons, settling in places like Texas, Oregon, California, and Colorado.

§ From 1861 to 1865, a terrible war was fought between the North and the South in the United States. It was called the Civil War. One of the primary reasons for the war was the issue of slavery. In 1862, President Abraham Lincoln declared all slaves free when he issued the executive order entitled the Emancipation Proclamation. Every slave was eventually freed by July of 1865.

§ The Statue of Liberty was a gift to America from France. It was unveiled in 1886, and thousands of people (like Sarah Jane) were in New York for the celebration.

§ Women were granted the right to vote in 1920 by the movement known as "women's suffrage." Men had been able to vote for hundreds of years prior to that.

§ In the 1930s, America went through a very difficult time known as the Great Depression. During this time, thousands of people were out of jobs. However, people (like Eleanor Jo's parents) worked hard to make sure their families had food to eat and clothes to wear.

§ In 1941, American entered World War II. Children (like Eleanor Jo) joined in the war effort by planting Victory gardens and raising money for the American Red Cross.

§ Modern-day families are researching their family trees in an attempt to learn more about their ancestors. This is a fun activity that parents, grandparents (like Grand Doll), and children (like Melanie Ann) can all participate in.

§ In the Eleanor Series, Grand Doll loves to tell stories. One of her favorite songs in this book is "I Love to

Tell the Story." This song was first a poem entitled "Tell Me the Old, Old Story." Arabella Catherine Hankey wrote the poem in 1867, when she was ill and was required to stay in bed. The poem is about the life and works of Jesus and the redemption that He provided for us.

Questions to Ponder

§ Why is it important to know about your family's heritage/legacy?

§ How much do you know about your family's history? Is there anything you don't know but wish you did?

§ What is your favorite family story?

§ What stories do you think people will tell about you one hundred years from now?

§ Has anyone in your family collected items from the past? If so, what are they?

§ If you could save one thing to pass on to your children and/or grandchildren, what would it be, and why?

§ Do you have a favorite grandparent (or aunt or uncle)? What makes that person so special to you?

§ Have you learned anything about America's history by listening to your family's stories?

§ What kind of parent do you think you will be someday? What will your children be like?

§ What does it mean to leave a legacy? What legacy do you hope to leave to your children and grandchildren?

What Is Love?

And now abide faith, hope, love, these three; but the greatest of these is love.

—1 Corinthians 13:13 NKJV

§ How are we commanded to love one another?

By this we know love, because He laid down His life for us. And we also ought to lay down our lives for the brethren. But whoever has the world's goods, and sees his brother in need, and shuts up his heart from him, how does the love of God abide in him? My little children, let us not love in word or in tongue, but in deed and in truth.

—1 John 3:16–18 NKJV

List some of the ways we can show the love of God in our daily living. For example, how does your family show love to one another? Can God's love be seen by the way you interact with and serve your parents, your brothers, your sisters, and the other members of your family?

Hint: First Corinthians 13:4 tells us, *Love suffers* [puts up with] *long and is kind; love does not envy* [become jealous]; *love does not parade itself; is not puffed up* [proud] (NKJV). Matthew 20:28 reminds us that *"the Son of Man did not come to be served, but to serve"* (NKJV). Always remember, love serves!

_____

_____

_____

_____

_____

_____

How does His love shine through us as we meet together in church or in school? And how about those we come in contact with in stores and restaurants? Give

some examples of how we can be more
loving in our attitudes and our actions. Our
attitudes are so very important: it's not only
what we do, but what we dwell on in our hearts and
minds. The Bible tells us, *For as he* [a man or woman]
thinks in his heart, so is he (Proverbs 23:7 NKJV).

_____

_____

_____

_____

Should we treat others whom we don't know very
well with the same respect we show to our own family
and friends? _____ Does "loving God" mean just
going to a church? Explain.

_____

_____

_____

_____

_____

What is the greatest commandment? Where can it be found in the New Testament?

Hint: Jesus was asked this question by one of the religious leaders, a Pharisee. It is also found in the Old Testament in Deuteronomy 6:5.

_____

_____

_____

_____

What do you think it means to love someone else as you love yourself? Are you "others minded"? In other words, do you think of someone else's needs or wants before your own? Give some examples.

_____

_____

_____

_____

_____

_____

Write a short story that describes ways to put others first.

A Challenge Question: The key verse in this story is 1 Corinthians 13:13, which says, *And now abide faith, hope, love, these three; but the greatest of these is love* (NKJV). Explain in your own words and from the Bible why you believe love is the greatest of the three. When using the Bible, give the scripture references.

Hint: How does the Bible say faith works? You can find a clue in Galatians 5:6.

_____

_____

_____

_____

_____

_____

_____

The greatest love is God's love. John 3:16 says, "*For God so loved the world that He gave His only begotten Son, that whoever believes in Him should not perish but have everlasting life*" (NKJV). God gave His very best, His own Son…and aren't you glad He did!

In John 15:13 we read, *"Greater love hath no man than this, that a man lay down his life for his friends"* (NKJV). Jesus bore our sins in His body on the cross and shed His precious blood as a sacrifice. He died and was raised from the dead so that we could become born-again children of God.

Another way to explain what Jesus did for us is to say that He took our unrighteousness (separation from God) and gave us His righteousness (right standing with God). This act of love is sometimes called "the great exchange."

Write your personal testimony of how you came to accept Jesus Christ as your own Savior and Lord.

_____

_____

_____

_____

_____

_____

_____

If you don't know Jesus, now would be a good time to think about what you have read and learned. He is just waiting for you to say yes to Him. You can pray something like this:

Yes, Jesus, I believe You shed Your precious blood on the cross for my sin. I believe You died and God raised You from the dead. I confess my sin to You and accept Your sacrifice for me. I now believe that You are my Savior and Lord and that I am a born-again child of God, adopted into Your very own family. Thank You, Jesus!

If you prayed this prayer...
WELCOME TO THE FAMILY OF GOD!

Record the date here: _____

Look up the definition for each of Grand Doll's legacies and find a scripture from the Bible that talks about each one.

§ Perseverance

_____

_____

_____

§ Courage

_____

_____

_____

§ Trust

_____

_____

_____

§ Being a Good Witness

_____

_____

_____

§ Hard Work

_____

_____

_____

§ Love

_____

_____

_____

Leaving a Legacy
Activity Ideas

§ Create a scrapbook, like Melanie Ann did. Collect photographs and other small items that can be placed in a book for future generations to look at and enjoy.

§ Use a box or a trunk to collect larger items (like dolls, stuffed animals, etc.) that you would like to pass down to your children.

§ If possible, spend an afternoon interviewing one of your grandparents (or an aunt or uncle). Ask specific questions about what life was like during his or her childhood, and then let him or her know how much you enjoyed hearing the stories.

§ Write an essay about an influential person in your family's history. Tell what impresses you most about this person.

§ Dress up like a character from American history, just like Grand Doll did as a child. Which one will you choose, and why?

§ Create a family tree. Locate as many names as possible. While researching your family tree, try to figure out if you're related to anyone famous from American history.

§ Keep a journal, writing down your daily activities.

§ Make a decision to be patriotic. Fall in love with America!

§ Write a letter to your future children and grandchildren, telling them about your life. Add important details, like the name of the president, the kind of car your parents drive, and other such things.

§ After reading the story and realizing that the greatest legacy we can receive or give is love, write down the names of one or two of your relatives or ancestors who you believe have handed down a particular legacy of love to you.

_____

_____

_____

_____

_____

_____

Scrapbooking is a popular pastime. You can spend hours creating a special keepsake that will last a lifetime. There are many places you can go to purchase scrapbook materials. If you are on a budget, here is an easy and inexpensive way to preserve your special memories.

§ Purchase a large photo album that has self-sticking covers on each page for inserting pictures and others items and momentos. Find an album that has sheets which are not divided into picture sizes.

§ Gather items from home, such as the following:
  • Photographs
  • Magazines from which to cut out words
  • Decorations (fabric, stickers, bows, wrapping paper, etc.)
  • Keepsakes (anything special that you want to keep and preserve: theater tickets, vacation postcards, ribbons you've won, dried flowers, etc.)

§ Find a large place to work.

§ Spread out all of the pictures you would like to use.

§ Spread out your keepsakes to see what you have.

- § Go through magazines and cut out words that would add meaning and flair to your book.
- § Arrange photographs in chronological order, adding pictures and other decorations as needed.
- § Be creative and, above all, enjoy working on your scrapbook!

Researching your ancestry is a great family project. Work with your parents or grandparents to make a "tree" of your family lineage. The Internet is a good place to begin searching for your ancestors, and you may also want to visit libraries that have a genealogy department.

Use the family tree on the next page to help you get started. Copy it onto another, larger piece of paper and see how far back you can go in your family line as you fill in the blanks. Who knows? You may discover that you are related to someone famous!

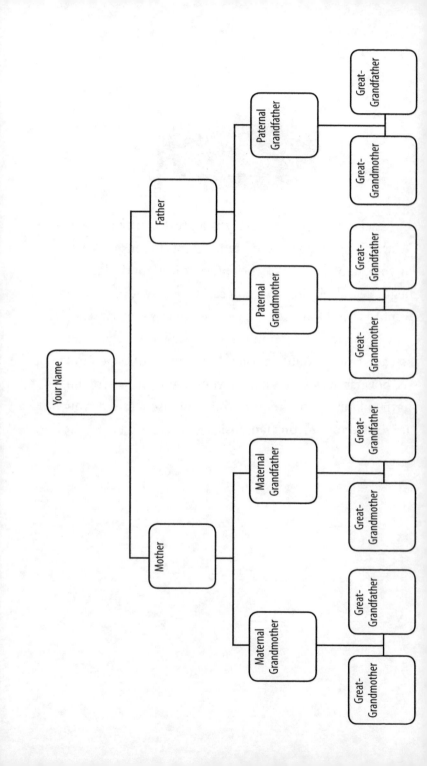

The Eleanor Series

E LEANOR CLARK CONCEIVED THE IDEA for *The Eleanor Series* while researching her family's rich American history. Motivated by her family lineage, which had been traced back to the early 17th century, a God-ordained idea emerged: the legacy left by her ancestors provided the perfect tool to reach today's children with the timeless truths of patriotism, godly character, and miracles of faith. Through her own family's stories, she instills in children a love of God and country, along with a passion for history. With that in mind, she set out to craft this collection of novels for the youth of today. Each story in *The Eleanor Series* focuses on a particular character trait and is laced with the pioneering spirit of one of Eleanor's true-to-life family members. These captivating stories span generations, are historically accurate, and highlight the nation's Christian heritage of faith. Twenty-first century readers—both children and parents—are sure to relate to these amazing character-building stories of young Americans while learning Christian values and American history.

LOOK FOR ALL OF THESE BOOKS IN THE ELEANOR SERIES:

Christmas Book—*Eleanor Jo: A Christmas to Remember*
ISBN-10: 0-9753036-6-X
ISBN-13: 978-0-9753036-6-5

Available in 2007

Book One—*Mary Elizabeth: Welcome to America*
ISBN-10: 0-9753036-7-8
ISBN-13: 978-0-9753036-7-2

Book Two—*Victoria Grace: Courageous Patriot*
ISBN-10: 0-9753036-8-6
ISBN-13: 978-0-9753036-8-9

Book Three—*Katie Sue: Heading West*
ISBN-10: 0-9788726-0-6
ISBN-13: 978-0-9788726-0-1

Book Four—*Sarah Jane: Liberty's Torch*
ISBN-10: 0-9753036-9-4
ISBN-13: 978-0-9753036-9-6

Book Five—*Eleanor Jo: The Farmer's Daughter*
ISBN-10: 0-9788726-1-4
ISBN-13: 978-0-9788726-1-8

Book Six—*Melanie Ann: A Legacy of Love*
ISBN-10: 0-9788726-2-2
ISBN-13: 978-0-9788726-2-5

Visit our Web site at: www.eleanorseries.com

About the Author

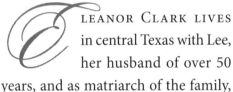 LEANOR CLARK LIVES in central Texas with Lee, her husband of over 50 years, and as matriarch of the family, she is devoted to her 5 children, 17 grandchildren, and 5 great grandchildren.

Born the daughter of a Texas sharecropper and raised in the Great Depression, Eleanor was a female pioneer in crossing economic, gender, educational, and corporate barriers. An executive for one of America's most prestigious ministries, Eleanor later founded her own highly successful consulting firm. Her appreciation of her American and Christian heritage comes to life along with her exciting and colorful family history in the youth fiction series *The Eleanor Series*.